# GEORGE O'CONNOR

# DIONYSOS

## THE NEW GOD

First Second

New York

IN THE TIME BEFORE TIME,
THERE WAS NOTHING, KAOS.

FROM KAOS CAME GAEA,
OUR GRANDMOTHER EARTH.
AND FROM GAEA CAME
OURANOS, THE SKY.

YOU KNOW THIS STORY ALREADY.

GAEA MADE OURANOS HER HUSBAND, AND HE FATHERED HER CHILDREN, THE TITANS.

A NEW TYPE OF GOD. THE GODS OF TIME.

AND THE TITANS OVERTHREW OURANOS.

OTHER CREATURES CAME INTO BEING. CYCLOPES, HEKATONCHIERES, NYMPHS, GIGANTES...

---HUMANS---

---AND ME.

THE FIRSTBORN CHILD OF KRONOS, KING OF THE TITANS, AND RHEA.

THE FIRST OF YET ANOTHER NEW TYPE OF GOD.

THE FIRST OLYMPIAN.

I WAS JUST A BABY THEN, WITH NO IDEA OF WHO I WAS OR MY TRUE SELF.

THE SHAPE I CHOSE FOR MYSELF HAD FAR MORE IN COMMON WITH HUMANS THAN THE COLOSSAL, TOWERING FORMS OF MY PARENTS.

WHY, I WONDER, DID I TAKE THAT HUMAN FORM?

HELPLESS, UNABLE TO PROTECT MYSELF.

THE CHILDREN OF OURANOS HAD OVERTHROWN HIM.

KRONOS WANTED TO TAKE NO CHANCE WITH HIS CHILDREN.

AND MY FATHER SWALLOWED ME WHOLE.

IN THE ENDLESS STARRY VOID THAT EXISTS IN THE GOD OF TIME, I STILL LIVED.

I AM IMMORTAL, AFTER ALL.

TIME PASSED, AND I GREW OLDER.

STUBBORNLY, I STILL HELD ON TO MY HUMAN FORM.

AND SO I LIVED, ALONE IN THE DARKNESS, FOR I DON'T KNOW HOW LONG.

ONE DAY, OR WHAT PASSED FOR A DAY IN THE VOID, SOMETHING NEW HAPPENED.

I SWAM OVER TO INSPECT THIS NEW ARRIVAL.

A BABY!

I DON'T KNOW IF HE HAD ALREADY TAKEN A HUMAN FORM BEFORE BEING SWALLOWED, OR IF I HAD SOMEHOW INSPIRED HIM.

BUT HE WAS HELPLESS AND ALONE, LIKE I HAD BEEN FOR SO LONG.

I RELAXED A BIT OF MY ASSUMED FORM, TO TAKE ON A LUMINESCENT QUALITY.

TO SHED SOME WARMTH AND LIGHT ON MY BROTHER AS HE SLUMBERED.

MORE TIME PASSED, AND MORE CHILDREN OF KRONOS JOINED US. I RELAXED MY FORM FURTHER.

MORE CHILDREN TO KEEP WARM.

FINALLY, A STONE CHILD CAME THROUGH. STILLBORN, I ASSUMED.

IT SEEMED TO MARK AN END—NO MORE CHILDREN FOLLOWED IT.

MORE TIME PASSED.

OCCASIONALLY THE SKY WOULD OPEN AND OBJECTS FROM THE WORLD OUTSIDE WOULD FALL THROUGH.

I WOULD MUSE UPON THESE OBJECTS, FABRICATE STORIES ABOUT THEM TO TELL MY SLUMBERING BROTHERS AND SISTERS.

SOMETIMES, AS THEY SLEPT, MY SIBLINGS WOULD TAKE ON OTHER FORMS.

SLEEPING THEIR WHOLE LIVES, I WONDERED WHAT SHAPES FILLED THEIR DREAMS?

MORE TIME PASSED, THE MOST YET.

THE SKY OPENED.

A FIGURE FELL THROUGH.

BUT NOT A CHILD THIS TIME.

OUR EYES LOCKED.

HE PULLED SOMETHING FROM HIS HEM AND THREW IT.

THE STARRY VOID SHUDDERED AND CONVULSED.

AND EVERYTHING WAS CAST OUT.

EVERYTHING BUT ME.

ALONE IN THE DARKNESS.

IN HIS EYES, I HAD SEEN SOMETHING OF MY FATHER. A HUNGER.

I TOOK A MOMENT TO CLOTHE MY FORM IN FLAMES.

AND I STEPPED OUT OF THE VOID...

...AND INTO THE WORLD.

BEFORE ME STRETCHED... EVERYTHING.

THE WHOLE WORLD. THE SKY, THE SEA, THE EARTH. THE MOUNTAINS, THE FIELDS, THE FORESTS.

EVEN PEOPLE.

I APPROACHED MY FAMILY, AWAKE AND STANDING UNDER A BLUE SKY.

HE TURNED.

THOSE EYES.

AWAKE FOR SO LONG, I HAD GREAT PATIENCE. PATIENCE ZEUS (FOR THAT WAS HIS NAME) DID NOT HAVE.

ZEUS IMMEDIATELY BEGAN A WAR AGAINST THE TITANS.

HAVING LIVED FOR SO LONG WITHOUT SPEAKING, I DIDN'T RAISE A VOICE TO PROTEST ZEUS'S PLAN.

THE WAR AGAINST THE TITANS ENDED. ZEUS AND MY SIBLINGS WERE VICTORIOUS. THEY SEALED THE TITANS IN PRISONS DEEP BENEATH THE EARTH'S CRUST.

THEY CLAIMED AS THEIR PALACE OLYMPUS, THE TALLEST MOUNTAIN LEFT STANDING, AND SET THEMSELVES AS RULERS OVER ALL WHO LIVED BELOW.

AND MY THOUGHTS TURNED TO THOSE CREATURES, ESPECIALLY THE HUMANS.

THEY HAD SUFFERED MUCH IN THIS CONFLAGRATION BETWEEN GODS.

THEY HUDDLED IN THE BLASTED LANDSCAPE, CULTIVATING SMALL FIRES TO KEEP THEMSELVES WARM, TRYING TO MAKE SENSE OF THIS STRANGE NEW WORLD THEY FOUND THEMSELVES IN.

ON OLYMPUS, I WAS ACCORDED A THRONE THAT I OCCUPIED, UNEASILY.

EVEN MORE TIME PASSED.

GODS MARRIED GODS, THEIR CHILDREN GODS THEMSELVES. OLYMPIANS, ALL, WITH ZEUS AS THEIR KING.

WITH THEIR NUMBERS, THEIR INTRIGUES AND INFIGHTING MULTIPLIED AS WELL.

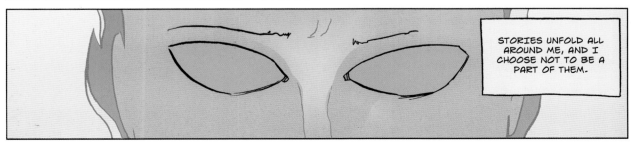

STORIES UNFOLD ALL AROUND ME, AND I CHOOSE NOT TO BE A PART OF THEM.

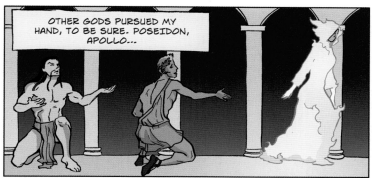

OTHER GODS PURSUED MY HAND, TO BE SURE. POSEIDON, APOLLO...

THE LESS SAID ABOUT PRIAPOS, THE BETTER.

I CHOSE TO REMAIN UNMARRIED, UNATTACHED.

AS THE GODS MULTIPLIED, SO, TOO, DID THE HUMANS.

THE OTHER OLYMPIANS ENCOURAGED THE HUMANS TO BUILD MAJESTIC TEMPLES IN THEIR HONOR.

ENORMOUS, GRANDIOSE STRUCTURES, HOUSING LARGER-THAN-LIFE COLOSSAL STATUES OF THE GODS.

I HAVE NO TEMPLES, OR VERY FEW.

I SATISFIED MYSELF WITH HUMBLER RECOGNITIONS.

IN EVERY HOUSE, IN EVERY HOME I DWELL.

THE FIRST PART OF EVERY MEAL, EVERY SACRIFICE, EVERY PRAYER IS OFFERED UP TO ME.

I BRING FAMILIES TOGETHER, GIVING LIGHT, WARMTH, AND COMFORT.

I KEEP THE DARKNESS AT BAY.

AROUND ME, A COMMUNION OF LOVED ONES, A PLACE TO SHARE WORRIES AND HOPES AND DREAMS.

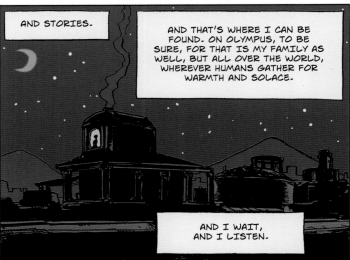

AND STORIES.

AND THAT'S WHERE I CAN BE FOUND. ON OLYMPUS, TO BE SURE, FOR THAT IS MY FAMILY AS WELL, BUT ALL OVER THE WORLD, WHEREVER HUMANS GATHER FOR WARMTH AND SOLACE.

AND I WAIT, AND I LISTEN.

AND ALL AROUND ME, STORIES ARE TOLD.

PRINCESS SEMELE? I'VE COME TO COMB YOUR HAIR.

OH, ALREADY? COME IN!

WHY ARE YOU SMILING SO, PRINCESS? YOU HAVE THE BLUSH OF YOUNG LOVE ON YOUR CHEEKS.

I DO? YES. I SUPPOSE I DO. I DO!

WHO IS IT? ONE OF THE COURTIERS?

NO, IT'S—NO, I SHOULDN'T TELL YOU, I—

TELL ME.

MY LOVER IS ZEUS, KING OF THE GODS HIMSELF.

OW, YOU PULLED MY HAIR!

HAHA. SURELY YOU MUST BE MISTAKEN OR DECEIVED. SOME FOOL PRETENDING TO BE ZEUS, TO WIN THE HEART OF A PRETTY G—

NO MISTAKE, FOR I HAVE SEEN HIM TAKE NEW FORM WITH MY OWN EYES! HE'S COME TO ME AS A SERPENT, AS A BEETLE, AS A BIRD!

NO, HE IS THE GOD ZEUS, AND HE LOVES ME TRUE. I KNOW BECAUSE HE HAS PROMISED ME ONE BOON, ONE WISH...

ANYTHING I WANT. HE HAS SWORN THIS ON THE RIVER STYX ITSELF!

AND THAT OATH IS UNBREAKABLE, EVEN TO THE GODS!

I WONDER HOW HE'LL COME TO ME TONIGHT. MAYBE AS A SWAN, OR A SHOWER OF GOLD...

HEHEHE.

WHY ARE YOU LAUGHING, NURSE? I DEMAND AN ANSWER!

IT'S JUST FUNNY— WELL, IT'S SAD, REALLY, I THINK, THAT YOU DON'T KNOW WHAT ZEUS *REALLY* LOOKS LIKE.

WHAT? OF COURSE I DO! HE IS TALL AND HANDSOME, WITH HAIR THE COLOR OF CLOUDS AND EYES THE COLOR OF THE SKY—

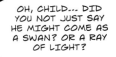

OH, CHILD... DID YOU NOT JUST SAY HE MIGHT COME AS A SWAN? OR A RAY OF LIGHT?

HE IS AN ALL-POWERFUL *GOD*. DO YOU THINK THE HANDSOME SHAPE HE PRESENTS TO YOU IS HIS TRUE FORM?

WHY, WHEN HE FIRST CAME TO HERA, QUEEN OF THE GODS, HE APPEARED AS A CUCKOO BIRD. WHO IS TO SAY THAT IS NOT HIS TRUE FORM?

MAYBE HE *IS* HERE WITH US NOW! MAYBE HE IS THIS ANT RIGHT HERE! HAHA!

NURSE, I DO NOT LIKE YOUR TONE. I WOULD HAVE YOU LEAVE ME, NOW.

I AM FINISHED ANYWAY, MY PRINCESS. BUT BEFORE I GO...

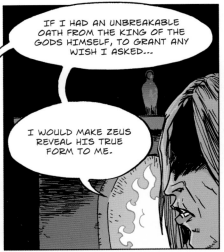

IF I HAD AN UNBREAKABLE OATH FROM THE KING OF THE GODS HIMSELF, TO GRANT ANY WISH I ASKED...

I WOULD MAKE ZEUS REVEAL HIS TRUE FORM TO ME.

ONLY THEN WOULD I TRULY KNOW IF HE LOVED ME OR NOT.

GOOD NIGHT, PRINCESS.

PRINCESS SEMELE? I'VE COME TO COMB YOUR HAIR.

ARE YOU SENILE AS WELL AS IMPERTINENT? GET OUT OF MY SIGHT, NURSE!

crunch!

LATER THAT NIGHT...

KRAKABOOM!

GUESS WHO?

WHY, IT MUST BE ZEUS...

OR WHOEVER YOU REALLY MAY BE.

WHOEVER I REALLY *MAY* BE? YOU'RE IN A FUNNY MOOD.

ZEUS? MY ONE WISH, THAT YOU SWORE TO ME? I'VE DECIDED WHAT I WANT.

ANYTHING.

I WANT TO SEE WHAT YOU *REALLY* LOOK LIKE. YOUR TRUE FORM.

NO, YOU DON'T.

WHAT? YES, I DO!

TRUST ME, YOU DO NOT. MY TRUE FORM... IS NOT FOR MORTAL EYES.

NOT FOR M—HOW CAN I TRUST YOU IF I CAN NEVER SEE WHAT YOU TRULY LOOK LIKE?! YOUR EVERY APPEARANCE TO ME IS A LIE!

THAT'S N—

YOU SWORE TO GRANT ME ONE WISH—ONE WISH ON THE RIVER STYX! AN UNBREAKABLE OATH! WELL, NOW I WILL USE THAT WISH!

ZEUS, I WISH FOR YOU TO REVEAL TO ME YOUR TRUE FORM!

SIIIGH... AS YOU WISH.

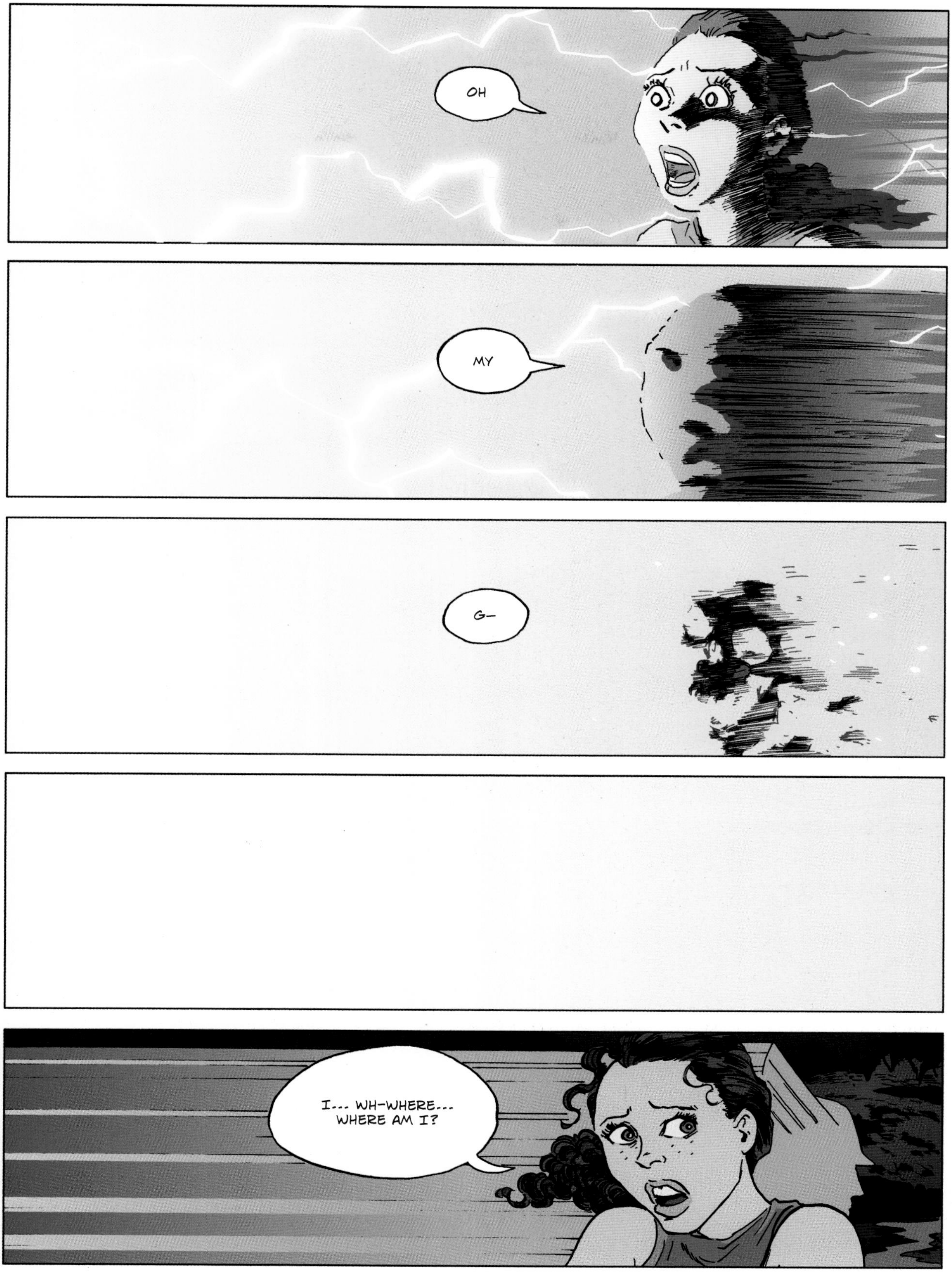
OH
MY
G–
I... WH-WHERE...
WHERE AM I?

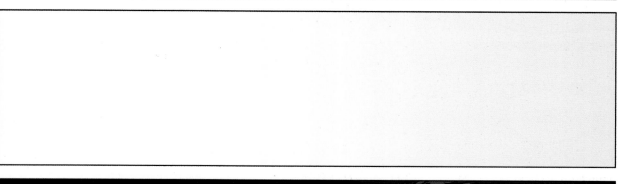

THE RIVER STYX.

THE SAME RIVER ZEUS SWORE AN UNBREAKABLE OATH TO YOU UPON.

HERE YOU WILL WAIT FOR CHARON THE BOATMAN TO TAKE YOU TO THE OTHER SIDE, TO THE UNDERWORLD...

THEN I?

WE GODS DON'T TAKE ON THESE STUNNING SHAPES JUST TO SEDUCE BEAUTIFUL YOUNG MORTALS...

WELL, MAYBE MY DAD DOES.

WE ARE BLAZING ENERGY, AND MORTALS JUST CAN'T ENDURE IT.

LOOK, I HAVE A ZILLION PLACES TO BE AT ONCE. I GOTTA SPLIT.

SORRY!

B-BUT I NEVER TOLD ZEUS...

...I'M PREGNANT.

YOU OKAY, POP?

THESE MORTALS... THEIR LIVES FLICKER SO BRIEFLY ALREADY.

ALL THAT SHE WAS... NOW JUST ASH...

WHEREEVER DID SHE GET THAT IDEA IN HER HEAD, DO YOU THINK, TO SEE YOU AS YOU REALLY ARE?

I CAN GUESS...

WAIT, LOOK, THERE. DO YOU SEE?

WHAT IS IT?

NOTHING YET.

IT'S ALL THAT REMAINS AFTER ALL THAT IS MORTAL WAS BURNED AWAY. A DIVINE SPARK...

BUT PERHAPS ONE DAY...

ZEUS FOLDED THAT DIVINE SPARK UNDER THE SKIN OF HIS OWN THIGH.

THERE THAT SPARK TOOK AND GREW TO TERM.

UNTIL IT WAS BORN, A CHILD FROM THE THIGH OF THE KING OF THE GODS.

THIS STRANGE BIRTH WAS ATTENDED ONLY BY HERMES, WHO WHISKED THE INFANT AWAY AT THE INSTANT OF DELIVERY.

21

WELL, THAT WAS EASILY THE WEIRDEST THING I'VE EVER SEEN, LITTLE ONE, AND BELIEVE YOU ME—I'VE SEEN SOME *STUFF.*

SHH, DON'T CRY. HERE, HAVE A GRAPE.

L-LORD HERMES!

GREETINGS, PRINCESS INO.

THERE'S TOO MUCH TO EXPLAIN, SO JUST UNDERSTAND THIS. YOU WILL NOT REMEMBER MY WORDS, BUT YOU WILL KNOW THIS TRUTH, LIKE A HALF-REMEMBERED DREAM.

YOUR SISTER, SEMELE, WHO DISAPPEARED? THIS IS HER BABY. IT IS IMPORTANT YOU RAISE THE CHILD AS YOU WOULD YOUR VERY OWN.

...

SHE HAS HER MOTHER'S EYES.

IN THE KINGDOM OF THEBES, DIONYSOS LIVED THE FIRST YEARS OF HER LIFE AS THE DAUGHTER OF INO.

HER TIME WITH INO'S FAMILY WAS A HAPPY TIME.

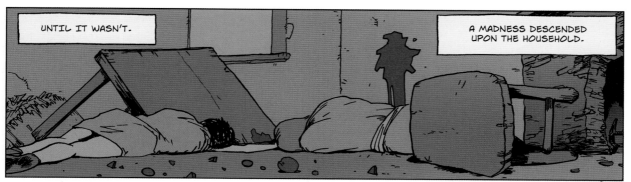

UNTIL IT WASN'T.

A MADNESS DESCENDED UPON THE HOUSEHOLD.

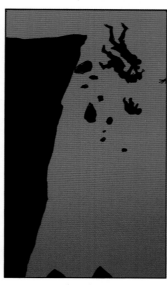

PHEW!

GOT HERE IN THE NICK OF TIME!

NO ONE COULD SAY WHENCE THE MADNESS CAME, BUT CONSIDERING THE FATES OF SEMELE, AND NOW HER SISTER, IT WAS ASSUMED THE CHILD OF ZEUS HAD ENEMIES.

THE DAUGHTER OF ZEUS WOULD NEED TO BE DISGUISED. HERMES WRAPPED HIMSELF IN ALL HIS GUILE AND SECRETED HER AWAY ONCE MORE, HE AS A SHEPHERD, THE CHILD AS A BABY RAM.

...SO I TOOK THE RAM TO THE LAST POSSIBLE PLACE THAT ANYONE IN THEIR RIGHT MIND WOULD *EVER* THINK OF LOOKING FOR A CHILD.

AND I FIGURE THAT'S **GOTTA** BE HERE, WITH YOU, SILENOS.

HEHE!

HEY, LITTLE ONE. COME SAY HI TO YER OL' UNCLE SILENOS.

OH, HERMES, I HAVE A FEELING THIS ONE IS GOING TO FIT IN WELL AROUND HERE.

ON MOUNT NYSA, WITH SILENOS, DIONYSOS LIVED HIS SECOND CHILDHOOD, WILD AND CAREFREE, THIS TIME AS THE **SON** OF ZEUS.

IT WAS A SAFE EXISTENCE, FOR AS HERMES HAD GUESSED, NO ONE WOULD THINK TO LOOK FOR A CHILD OF ZEUS AMONG THE SATYRS.

DIONYSOS MAY HAVE LOOKED SOFT, BUT HE GREW UP WITH LEOPARDS AS HIS PLAYMATES.

AND ON NYSA, DIONYSOS FELL IN LOVE FOR THE FIRST TIME.

AMPELOS, LOOK! WATCH THIS SNAKE.

SEE HOW IT BECOMES ADDLED AFTER SUCKING THE JUICE FROM THIS SPOILED GRAPE?

HA, OF COURSE! THE TASTE MUST BE AWFUL!

I THINK IT'S MORE THAN THAT.

IF THE TASTE IS SO AWFUL, WHY DOES THE SERPENT KEEP RETURNING TO IT?

IT GIVES ME AN IDEA. HERE, TRY THIS.

BLEAH!

IT TASTES *HORRIBLE!* I WAS RIGHT!

OH, WELL, HAND IT BACK, THEN. I'LL GET RID OF IT IF IT'S SO TERRIBLE.

MMM, I DIDN'T SAY THAT...

WHAT ARE YOU TWO RAPSCALLIONS GIGGLING ABOUT?

DIONYSOS HAS MADE AN AMAZING DISCOVERY! A MAGICAL ELIXIR, TO RIVAL THE NECTAR OF THE GODS!

TRY SOME!

THIS SMELLS FUNNY. KINDA GROSS.

JUST A SIP!

Sip!

poing!

GULPAGLUGGLUG!

26

I THINK HE LIKES IT!

oohoowoohoo woohoowoohoowoohoowoohoo

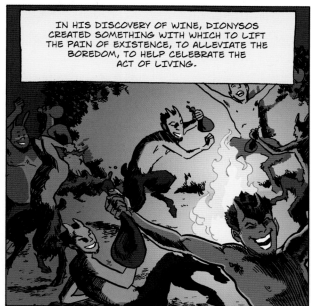

IN HIS DISCOVERY OF WINE, DIONYSOS CREATED SOMETHING WITH WHICH TO LIFT THE PAIN OF EXISTENCE, TO ALLEVIATE THE BOREDOM, TO HELP CELEBRATE THE ACT OF LIVING.

AND, IF ONE IS NOT CAREFUL, MAYBE A WISH FOR DEATH THE NEXT MORNING.

HOW'S SILENOS FEELING?

HE SAYS HIS HEAD FEELS LIKE ATHENA HERSELF IS TRYING TO BREAK OUT OF IT. SO, BETTER THAN HE WAS, I'D SAY.

I WARNED HIM. MY GIFT NEEDS TO BE TAKEN IN MODERATION.

SILENOS HAS NEVER EXACTLY BEEN ONE FOR MODERATION. HAHAHA!

AMPELOS, DO YOU REMEMBER WHEN I CAME HERE?

KINDA? I WAS A LITTLE KID THEN.

I REMEMBER LORD HERMES HIMSELF GAVE YOU TO OL' SILENOS. HE SAID WE HAD TO KEEP YOU SAFE.

HOW COME?

WELL, IT'S JUST... SOMETIMES AT NIGHT... WHEN I LAY MY HEAD ON THE EARTH... I HEAR VOICES.

WELL, ONE VOICE. SOMETIMES I THINK IT'S THE EARTH HERSELF... SOMETIMES... I THINK IT'S JUST ME.

WHAT DOES THIS VOICE SAY?

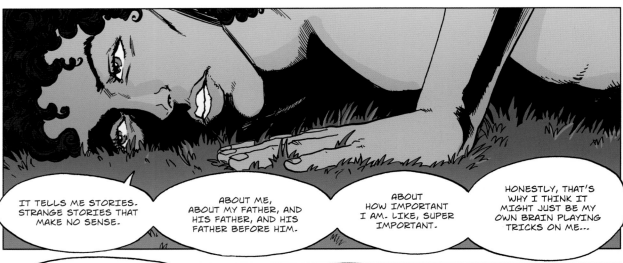

IT TELLS ME STORIES. STRANGE STORIES THAT MAKE NO SENSE.

ABOUT ME, ABOUT MY FATHER, AND HIS FATHER, AND HIS FATHER BEFORE HIM.

ABOUT HOW IMPORTANT I AM. LIKE, SUPER IMPORTANT.

HONESTLY, THAT'S WHY I THINK IT MIGHT JUST BE MY OWN BRAIN PLAYING TRICKS ON ME...

BUT THE VOICE TELLS ME... I WAS THINKING...

I LOVE IT HERE WITH SILENOS, WITH THE SATYRS, WITH *YOU*. BUT... I NEED TO GROW.

DIO, YOU WERE DELIVERED TO US BY A *FREAKING OLYMPIAN*. WE'VE ALWAYS KNOWN THAT YOU WERE MEANT FOR BIGGER THINGS!

WE SATYRS KEPT YOU SAFE AND HIDDEN AS YOU GREW, BUT IT'S TIME YOU FIND YOUR BIGGER PLACE IN THIS WORLD. AND THIS WINE? IT CAN HELP YOU DO IT.

AND, BUDDY, WE'RE GONNA HELP YOU MAKE WINE!

THE SATYRS TURNED ALL THEIR ATTENTIONS TO THE MAKING OF WINE, GATHERING EVERY GRAPE THEY COULD FIND ON MOUNT NYSA.

THEY WERE DRIVEN, INSANELY SO, EVEN. BUT BEING SATYRS, STILL WILD...

...STILL CARELESS.

AMPELOS, COME ON! WE'VE SCOURED THIS VINE FOR GRAPES!

HOLD ON!

29

WE DON'T NEED *EVERY* GRAPE!

SAYS YOU!

I CAN... ALMOST...

OH, DIONYSOS...

...I'M SORRY.

IT WAS HAPPENING AGAIN.

PEOPLE WERE DYING AROUND DIONYSOS.

HEARTBROKEN, MAD WITH GRIEF, DIONYSOS WANDERED OUT INTO THE DESERT, TO FIND AN ANSWER TO THE UNKNOWABLE.

THANK YOU, HEBE.

DESPITE HIS FATHER'S CLUMSY ATTEMPTS TO HIDE IT FROM ME, DIONYSOS IS CLEARLY A CHILD OF ZEUS.

THE BOY SEEMS INTENT ON BEING NOTICED. HE MAY ONLY BE HALF-OLYMPIAN, BUT HE OBVIOUSLY HAS SOME LEVEL OF DIVINE POWER.

BUT I WONDER, PERHAPS THESE MADNESSES THAT OCCUR ABOUT HIM, THAT PLAGUE HIM?

IS IT RIDICULOUS TO SUPPOSE, PERHAPS, THAT HE HIMSELF IS UNWITTINGLY THE CAUSE? PERHAPS THIS SON OF ZEUS... IS A GOD OF MADNESS?

OKAY, THE THING WITH HIS MOTHER, YES, THAT WAS TOTALLY ME.

BUT THAT WAS ENOUGH. I WAS SATISFIED.

THE REST OF HIS MISFORTUNES, WELL...

I FEAR THIS DIONYSOS MAY HAVE TOO MUCH OF HIS FATHER IN HIM.

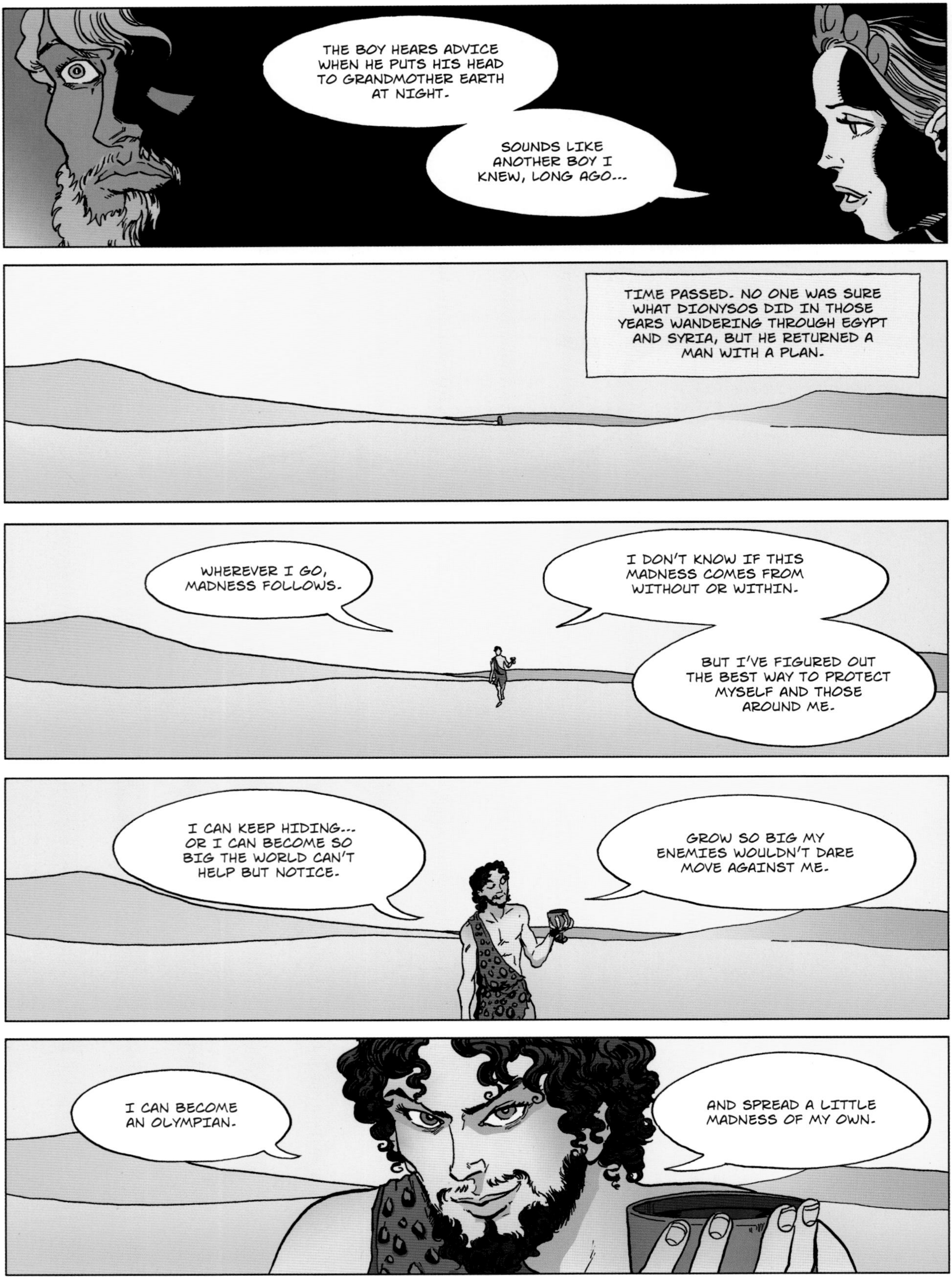

THE BOY HEARS ADVICE WHEN HE PUTS HIS HEAD TO GRANDMOTHER EARTH AT NIGHT.
SOUNDS LIKE ANOTHER BOY I KNEW, LONG AGO...
TIME PASSED. NO ONE WAS SURE WHAT DIONYSOS DID IN THOSE YEARS WANDERING THROUGH EGYPT AND SYRIA, BUT HE RETURNED A MAN WITH A PLAN.
WHEREVER I GO, MADNESS FOLLOWS.
I DON'T KNOW IF THIS MADNESS COMES FROM WITHOUT OR WITHIN.
BUT I'VE FIGURED OUT THE BEST WAY TO PROTECT MYSELF AND THOSE AROUND ME.
I CAN KEEP HIDING... OR I CAN BECOME SO BIG THE WORLD CAN'T HELP BUT NOTICE.
GROW SO BIG MY ENEMIES WOULDN'T DARE MOVE AGAINST ME.
I CAN BECOME AN OLYMPIAN.
AND SPREAD A LITTLE MADNESS OF MY OWN.

DIONYSOS WAS A MAN—ER, A GOD—WITH A MISSION.

AND WE SATYRS WERE THERE WITH HIM. WE HEADED OUT FROM MOUNT NYSA TO SPREAD THE WORD OF WINE.

THINGS WENT ROCKY AT FIRST.

OUTSIDE OF ATHENS, DIO TAUGHT A MAN NAMED IKARIOS THE SECRET OF HOW TO MAKE WINE.

IKARIOS WAS TO TEACH OTHERS ABOUT WINE, AND HE SHOWED THE MAGICAL ELIXIR TO SOME SHEPHERDS.

THEY DRANK TOO MUCH AND THOUGHT THEY HAD BEEN POISONED.

AND, WELL, LET'S JUST SAY, WINE DIDN'T TAKE IN ATHENS.

BUT THAT DIDN'T COMPARE TO OUR RECEPTION IN THRACE.

I AM LYCURGUS, KING OF THESE LANDS.

WE THRACIANS ARE STEADY AND RESOLUTE, LIKE THE OAK. SOBER AND SURE.

I'VE HEARD TELL OF YOUR "MAGICAL" DRINK THAT CAUSES MADNESS.

THERE IS NO PLACE IN THRACE FOR WINE, OR FOR THE GAGGLE OF UNRULY SATYRS WHO CARRY IT.

I HEAR YOU, LYSEY— CAN I CALL YOU LYSEY? LOVE YOUR MUSTACHE, BY THE WAY.

ANYWAY, LYSEY, HOW ABOUT YOU PROMISE JUST TO LET US THROUGH YOUR LANDS...

AND WE PROMISE NOT TO MAKE FUN OF YOUR MUSTACHE.

TOO MUCH.

WHAT DO YOU SAY?

LYCURGUS AND HIS ARMY DROVE US INTO THE SEA.

AND IT'S AROUND THAT TIME THAT I GOT KIDNAPPED.

WELL, KIDNAPPED MIGHT BE TOO STRONG A WORD.

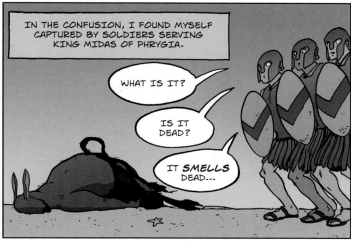

IN THE CONFUSION, I FOUND MYSELF CAPTURED BY SOLDIERS SERVING KING MIDAS OF PHRYGIA.

WHAT IS IT?

IS IT DEAD?

IT **SMELLS** DEAD...

I WAS HELD PRISONER FOR MONTHS AND INTERROGATED IN DISMAL CONDITIONS.

SERVANTS! MORE FOOD FOR OUR HUNGRY FRIEND HERE!

AFTER A LONG CAPTIVITY, DIONYSOS FOUND ME AND DEMANDED MY RELEASE.

AW, DO I HAVE TO GO?

I CAN'T THANK YOU ENOUGH FOR THE HOSPITALITY YOU SHOWED SILENOS.

HE WAS A DELIGHT! SUCH STORIES HE WOULD TELL!

HE TELLS ME YOU CAN TURN GRAPE JUICE INTO THIS WONDERFUL ELIXIR WITH A TOUCH!

THIS IS TRUE.

MY! MAYBE, AS A THANK-YOU, COULD YOU MAKE IT SO THAT **MY** TOUCH HAS THE POWER TO TRANSFORM THINGS AS WELL?

HMM, WELL, WHAT WOULD YOU LIKE YOUR TOUCH TO TURN THINGS INTO?

REALLY? WOW! WHAT **WOULD** I WANT TO CREATE WITH MY TOUCH? WAIT, I KNOW! I'D WANT MY TOUCH TO TURN EVERYTHING INTO—

GOLD!

HAHAHA! SUCH A GREAT IDEA I HAD! I'LL BE THE RICHEST KING IN THE WORLD!

TOO BAD ABOUT MY SERVANTS... THOUGH THEY DO MAKE FOR NICE STATUES.

SOLID-GOLD VASE?

DON'T MIND IF I DO!

HAHA! BOY, ALL THIS GOLD MAKING SURE HAS GIVEN ME AN APPETITE!

OW!

WHAT THE...

OW!!

HMMM...

BOY, I REALLY AM HUNGRY.

HUH.

I'VE MADE A HUGE MISTAKE.

HA, ZEUS, COME OVER. WE WERE JUST DISCUSSING THIS WAYWARD SON OF YOURS.

SON?

THIS HALF-MORTAL. DIONYSOS.

I'M NOT SURE ABOUT THIS ONE, ZEUS. CONFERRING DIVINE GIFTS UPON IDIOT KINGS, WAGING WARS ON OTHERS...

THAT DIDN'T GO SO WELL FOR HIM. THE BOY AND HIS... ARMY WERE LITERALLY DRIVEN INTO MY REALM.

HE WAS? IS HE ALL RIGHT?

YOU JEST, POSEIDON. BUT I WORRY ABOUT DIONYSOS. THE THINGS HE DOES... I WONDER, IS THERE A METHOD TO HIS MADNESS?

WORRY NOT, FATHER. THE BOY IS FINE. DIONYSOS IS JUST DISCOVERING HIMSELF, TESTING HIMSELF.

DARE I SAY, FORGING HIMSELF?

WHEN HE WAS DRIVEN TO THE SEA, DIONYSOS TOOK REFUGE WITH THETIS, SHE WHO SHELTERED ME WHEN I WAS CAST FROM OLYMPUS AS A BABE.

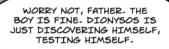

YOU TWO REMEMBER THETIS, DON'T YOU, FATHER, UNCLE?

THERE TO BIDE HIS TIME. RECOVER. AND AWAIT THE PERFECT TIME TO STRIKE BACK.

AND NOT A MOMENT SOONER.

AFTER ALL, A BLADE PULLED TOO SOON FROM THE FORGE WILL SURELY BREAK.

THEBES

HERE IS THE PRISONER, KING PENTHEUS.

WE BELIEVE HE IS ASSOCIATED WITH--- THE TROUBLEMAKER.

SPEAK, KNAVE! IDENTIFY YOURSELF!

GREETINGS, O KING, MY NAME IS ACOETES.

I'M FROM A HUMBLE FAMILY, BUT UNTIL RECENTLY I HAD THE GOOD FORTUNE TO FIND WORK AS A MARINER-FOR-HIRE.

HMM, PIRATE, YOU MEAN.

I'VE BEEN HEARING THINGS, DISTURBING THINGS, ABOUT THIS MAN WITH WHOM YOU TRAVEL.

TELL ME... ABOUT DIONYSOS.

I'LL TELL YOU, O KING...

BUT DIONYSOS IS NO MERE MAN...

MY COMPANIONS FOUND HIM DOZING ON A RIVERBANK, IN A KIND OF STUPOR.

THEY FIGURED HIM SOME SORT OF FOREIGN-BORN PRINCE OR SOMETHING, SOMEONE WHO MIGHT FETCH A RICH RANSOM.

HUH?

GOOD MORNING.

OH, UH, HI?

THEY BROUGHT HIM ABOARD THE SHIP IN CHAINS.

HE WAS SO BEAUTIFUL, I COULD SEE HIM FOR WHAT HE WAS IMMEDIATELY.

THIS IS NO PRINCE, NO RICH MAN'S SON! SURELY, THIS IS A *GOD* YOU'VE BROUGHT ABOARD OUR SHIP IN FETTERS!

SHUT YOUR YAP, HELMSMAN, AND TAKE YOUR POST!

WE PULL UP ANCHOR, AND AFTER WE REACH SEA WE'LL INTERROGATE OUR PRISONER AND FIND OUT FROM WHERE TO CLAIM OUR RANSOM!

YOU FOOL! THE AWARD YOU'LL RECEIVE FOR ABDUCTING A GOD WILL NOT BE RICHES!

I WILL NOT STAND BY THIS BLASPHEMY!

MY MUTINY WAS QUICKLY SUPPRESSED.

AUGHN!

ROWERS, TO POSITION! HOIST THE SAILS!

I WANT OFF THIS COAST BEFORE ANYONE NOTICES THIS PRETTY PRINCE GONE!

AND ONCE WE'RE TO SEA WE'LL THROW THIS TRAITOROUS HELMSMAN TO THE SHARKS!

UH, GUYS, CAN YOU KEEP IT DOWN?

MY HEAD IS POUNDING...

OH, HE'S DECIDED TO JOIN US, OUR PRETTY FOREIGN GUEST!

SO WHERE DO YOU CALL HOME, MY PRETTY LITTLE CAPTIVE? A MANSION OR CASTLE, NO DOUBT.

SOME OF MY MEN, THEY THOUGHT YOU WERE A WOMAN AT FIRST GLANCE, YOU'RE SO PRETTY.

AND THIS IDIOT EVEN THOUGHT YOU WERE A GOD.

THAT IDIOT?

YEAH, THAT'S RIGHT. THIS IDIOT HERE.

OH.

WELL, HE'S RIGHT.

I COULD FEEL IT, EVEN FROM MY SPOT, LYING ON THE DECK.

THE SHIP STOPPED DEAD IN THE WATER. AT FULL SAILS.

WHAT HAPPENED? WHY DID WE STOP?

BELOW, ON THE OAR DECKS, I HEARD SCREAMS.

BY THE GODS...

NOT THE GODS.

JUST ME.

AAAARRRRGH!

A SUDDEN JUNGLE OVERTOOK THE DECK.

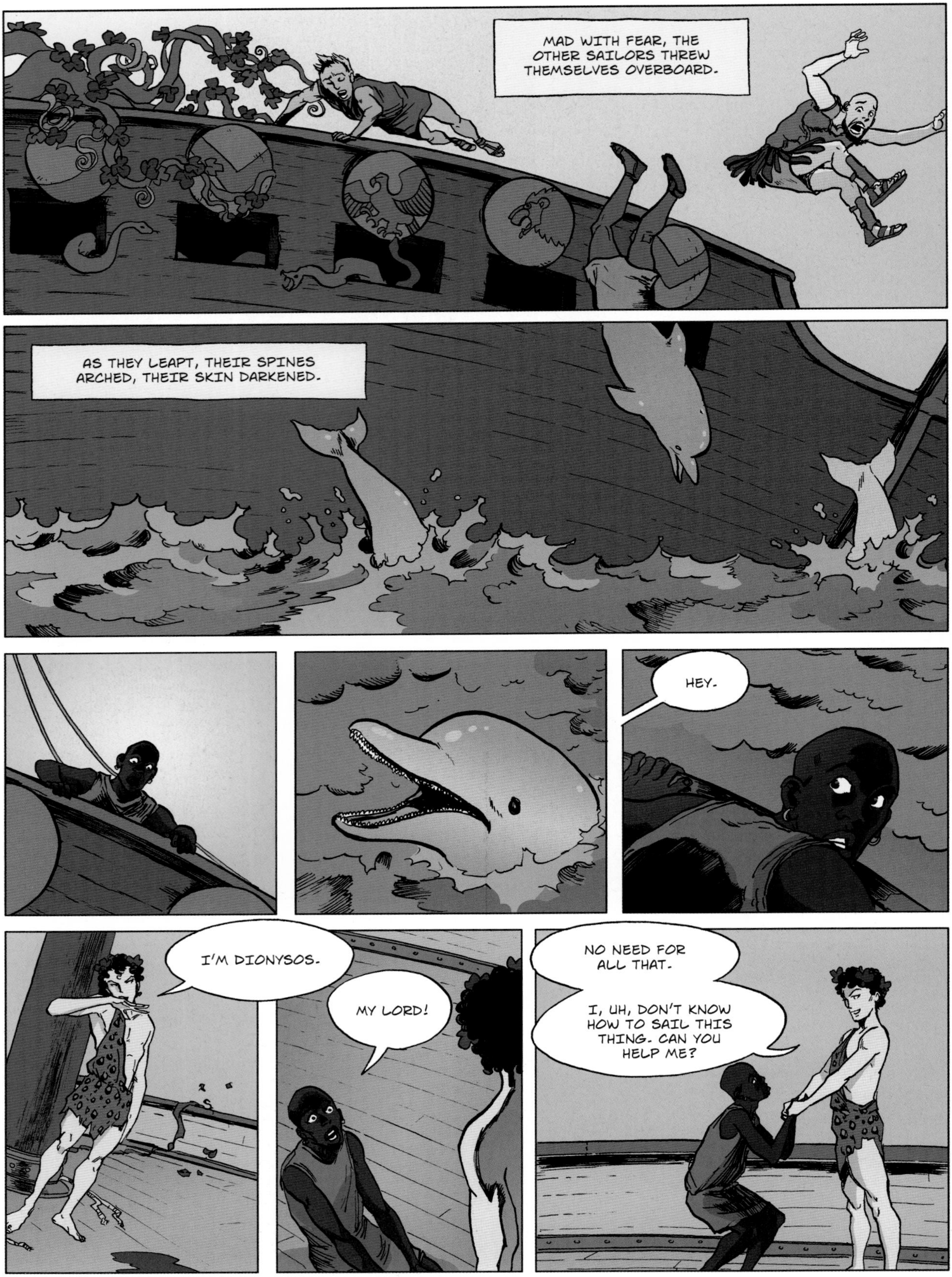
MAD WITH FEAR, THE OTHER SAILORS THREW THEMSELVES OVERBOARD.
AS THEY LEAPT, THEIR SPINES ARCHED, THEIR SKIN DARKENED.
HEY.
I'M DIONYSOS.
MY LORD!
NO NEED FOR ALL THAT.
I, UH, DON'T KNOW HOW TO SAIL THIS THING. CAN YOU HELP ME?

AND THAT IS HOW I BECAME BLESSED TO ENTER THE SERVICE OF DIONYSOS.

I'VE HEARD ENOUGH!

THIS DIONYSOS, THIS TROUBLE HE'S CAUSING, STIRRING UP THE RABBLE—HIS KIND IS NOT WELCOME IN THEBES.

TAKE THIS ZEALOT AWAY. TORTURE HIM!

YOUR GOD CAN'T HELP YOU NOW.

SIRE, IN THE CITY...

THE WOMEN...

THE WOMEN ARE UPRISING...

I DON'T UNDERSTAND IT.

THIS LUNATIC MOB DIONYSOS HAS ASSEMBLED AROUND HIMSELF, THESE INSANE DEEDS HE'S COMMITTING...

DOES HE UNDERSTAND ALL THE THINGS I DID TO KEEP HIM SECRET, KEEP HIM SAFE?

I UNDERSTAND TRYING TO PROTECT YOUR CHILD—BELIEVE ME I DO—BUT I THINK DIONYSOS IS TRYING TO FIND A PLACE FOR HIMSELF IN THE WORLD.

WITH SO MUCH OF THE COSMOS ALREADY SPOKEN FOR, HE FINDS HIS FOLLOWERS AMONGST THOSE WHO HAVE TENDED NOT TO BE COUNTED.

HMM.

THE WAY HE MADE THOSE VINES GROW. THOSE BEAUTIFUL SPROUTS OF CURLING GREEN...

IT REMINDS ME OF OUR DAUGHTER, ZEUS.

I MISS PERSEPHONE, TOO, DEMETER.

SPRING IS NEARLY UPON US. SHE'LL BE BACK SOON.

WOW, THAT WAS SURPRISINGLY CATHARTIC! ANYTHING TO ADD, ARES?

FEH, I JUST WISH THERE WAS A BIG FIGHT.

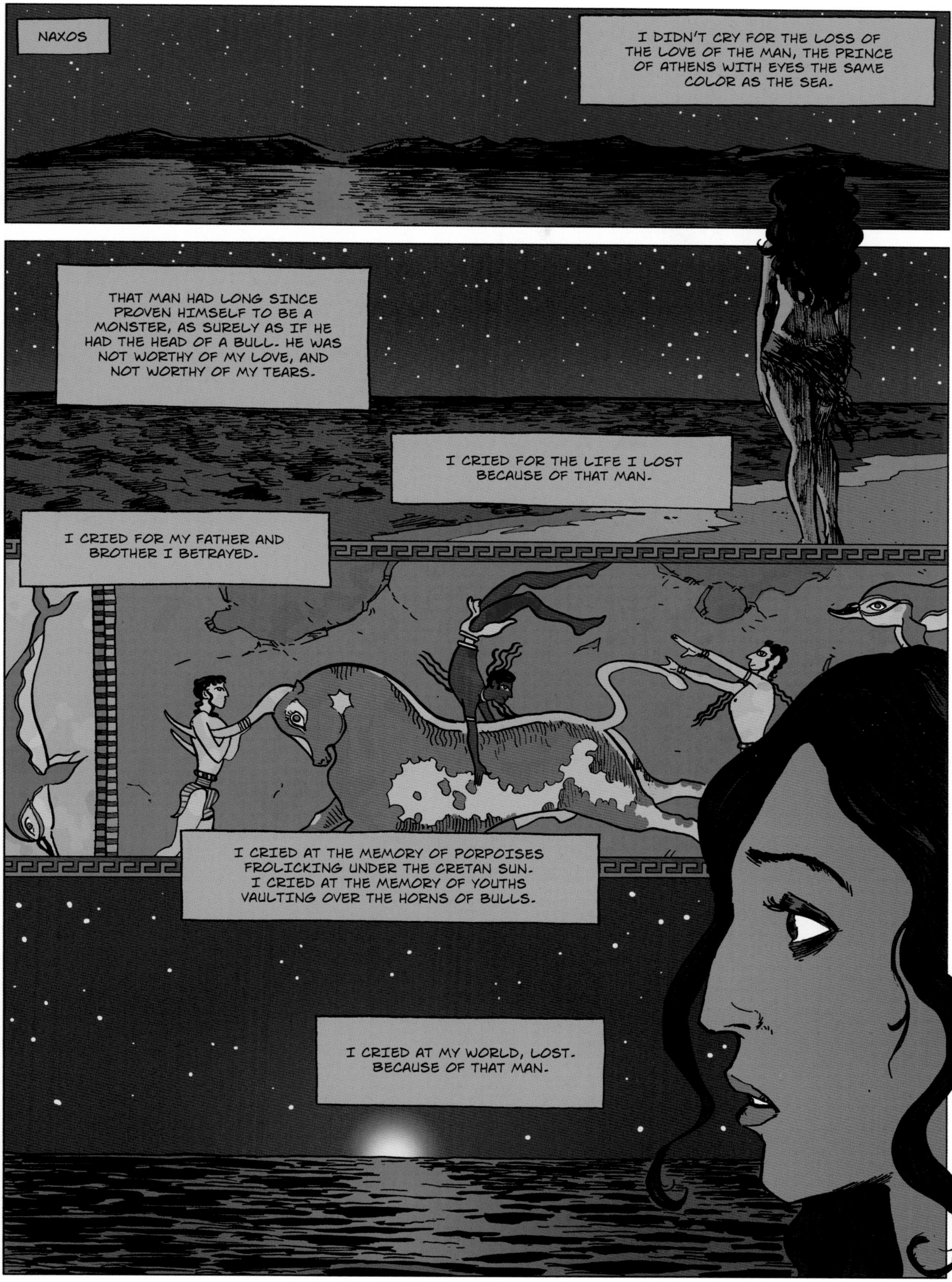
NAXOS
I DIDN'T CRY FOR THE LOSS OF THE LOVE OF THE MAN, THE PRINCE OF ATHENS WITH EYES THE SAME COLOR AS THE SEA.
THAT MAN HAD LONG SINCE PROVEN HIMSELF TO BE A MONSTER, AS SURELY AS IF HE HAD THE HEAD OF A BULL. HE WAS NOT WORTHY OF MY LOVE, AND NOT WORTHY OF MY TEARS.
I CRIED FOR THE LIFE I LOST BECAUSE OF THAT MAN.
I CRIED FOR MY FATHER AND BROTHER I BETRAYED.
I CRIED AT THE MEMORY OF PORPOISES FROLICKING UNDER THE CRETAN SUN. I CRIED AT THE MEMORY OF YOUTHS VAULTING OVER THE HORNS OF BULLS.
I CRIED AT MY WORLD, LOST. BECAUSE OF THAT MAN.

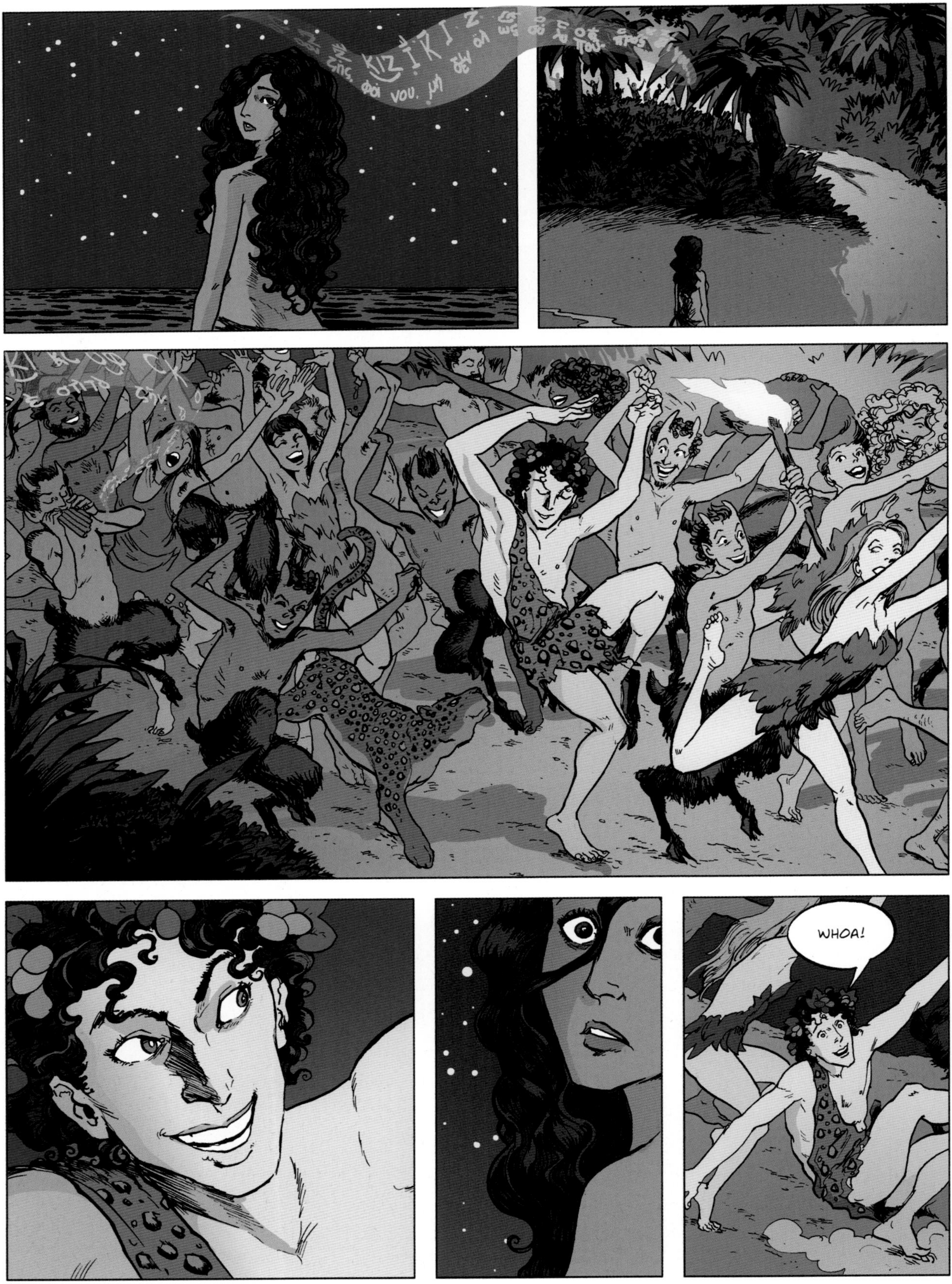
WHOA!

HEY! YOU'RE— YOU'RE HERE!

I AM.

THIS IS SO WILD. A VOICE TOLD ME I'D FIND SOMEONE—OH, YEAH, I TOTALLY HEAR VOICES.

VOICES?

YEAH, NOT LIKE I'M CRAZY. LIKE GRANDMOTHER EARTH, SHE SPEAKS TO ME!

THE EARTH... SPEAKS TO YOU?

YEAH! MAYBE? THE VOICE TOLD ME TO COME TO NAXOS, I HAVE SOMEONE TO MEET THERE. AND I'M LIKE, COOL! WELL, MAYBE THE VOICE IS ME, AND IT'S TELLING ME TO GO TO NAXOS BECAUSE NAXOS KINDA SOUNDS LIKE NYSOS—

NOT REALLY.

AND I'M DIONYSOS, BY THE WAY—HI!

ARIADNE.

HI! SO ANYWAY, THE VOICE IN MY HEAD, WHICH IS MAYBE GRANDMOTHER EARTH OR IS MAYBE JUST ME, THIS VOICE TELLS ME TO COME TO NAXOS BECAUSE I HAVE SOMEONE TO MEET HERE!

AND HERE I AM!

AND HERE YOU ARE!

SO, UH, WHY ARE YOU SMILING?

AM I?

NO REASON.

DIONYSOS AND I WERE WED THAT VERY NIGHT.

I'D ALREADY LOST AN ENTIRE WORLD ONCE. AND FOR TOO LONG AFTER THAT, MY ONLY WORLD WAS NAXOS.

A WHOLE NEW WORLD OPENED UP FOR ME AT DIONYSOS'S SIDE.

AND LIFE IS TOO SHORT TO WAIT, YOU KNOW?

SILENOS!

LOOK AT THE HAPPY COUPLE! THIS OLD GOAT COULDN'T BE HAPPIER FOR YOU CRAZY KIDS!

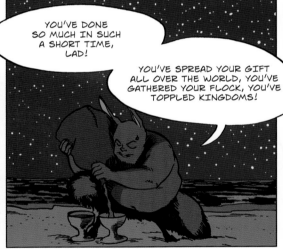

YOU'VE DONE SO MUCH IN SUCH A SHORT TIME, LAD!

YOU'VE SPREAD YOUR GIFT ALL OVER THE WORLD, YOU'VE GATHERED YOUR FLOCK, YOU'VE TOPPLED KINGDOMS!

YOU'VE EVEN FOUND LOVE!

WHAT ON GRANDMOTHER EARTH WILL YOU DO NEXT?

I'M GLAD YOU ASKED, SILENOS.

I LOOK AROUND ME, AND I CAN'T HELP BUT NOTICE THOSE WHO AREN'T WITH US ANYMORE.

SILENOS, OLD MAN, I'M GOING TO CONQUER DEATH.

MARRIED? REALLY? ALL OF A SUDDEN DIONYSOS IS MARRIED NOW? TO WHOM?

APHRODITE, WAS THIS YOUR DOING?

MOST ASSUREDLY NOT. YOUNG LOVE CAN SPRING UP ANYWHERE AND GROW UNCHECKED, LIKE A WEED... OR A VINE.

BUT SHE'S A LOVELY GIRL, ZEUS. A CRETAN PRINCESS. YOU SHOULD BE VERY HAPPY FOR THEM.

AND IT WAS A BIT RUSTIC FOR MY TASTES, BUT BY ALL ACCOUNTS IT WAS A LOVELY WEDDING.

WEDDINGS AREN'T USUALLY MY THING, BUT I HAVE TO AGREE.

IT'S WHAT THEY WANTED, WHAT THEY CHOSE. YOU HAVE TO RESPECT THAT.

I THINK THEY COULD HAVE USED BETTER MUSIC. MAYBE I'LL GO DOWN THERE AND PLAY FOR THEM—

APOLLO, NO.

IT'S JUST... THEY JUST MET! THAT SAME NIGHT!

WHAT IF IT'S A MISTAKE?

APHRODITE, WITH YOUR POWERS, COULD YOU...?

DO NOT ASK THIS OF ME, O KING OF GODS.

AFFAIRS OF THE HEART ARE HARD TO NAVIGATE. AN UNHAPPY MARRIAGE CAN LAST YEARS, BUT TRUE LOVE MAY BLOOM IN AN INSTANT.

IN ORDER FOR DIONYSOS TO MATURE, HIS MISTAKES, AND HIS TRIUMPHS, MUST BE HIS OWN.

THRACE, AGAIN

I'VE HEARD WHAT YOU'VE DONE IN ATHENS. IN BOEOTIA.

IN THEBES, PENTHEUS TORN TO SHREDS BY AN ARMY OF HIS OWN WOMEN.

AND DON'T YOU SUPPOSE HEARING SOMETHING LIKE THAT WOULD MAKE YOU INCLINED TO GIVE ME FREE PASSAGE?

FUNNY.

WE THRACIANS HAVE NO ROOM FOR YOU OR YOUR WICKED DRINK.

I GET IT, LYSEY. I REALLY DO. I TRIED WITH YOU ALREADY; MY GIFT IS NOT FOR EVERYONE.

MY CREW AND I ARE JUST PASSING THROUGH, ON OUR WAY TO THE UNDERWORLD.

OH, YOU'LL GET TO THE UNDERWORLD, BUT NOT HOW YOU'D LIKE!

ATTACK!

YES!

FINALLY!

50

UNGH!

GROWL

HAHAHAHA!

ERK!

AIEEE!

FALL BACK! RETREAT!

RETREAT? IN MY OWN KINGDOM?! NEVER!

COME ON, THEN!

COME ON!!

THE KING IS MAD!

—CUT THEM OFF!

—ATTACKING HIS OWN LEGS—

—GONNA BE SICK!

OH, COME ON!

SOLDIERS OF THRACE, YOU'VE SEEN THE MADNESS THAT BEFELL YOUR KING? ONE MINUTE WE WERE TALKING, THE NEXT HE ATTACKED HIS OWN LEGS??

THAT MADNESS? THAT CAME FROM *ME.*

NOW, I INVITE YOU— JUST STAND ASIDE AND LET MY FOLLOWERS AND I THROUGH, UNMOLESTED.

OR... YOU COULD BAR MY WAY...

...AND JOIN YOUR KING.

AH.

YOU SHOULD HAVE A DRINK, LYCURGUS.

IT HELPS WITH THE PAIN.

THE GATES OF THE UNDERWORLD

LET THIS TORCH LIGHT YOUR WAY, DIONYSOS.

I WOULD GO WITH YOU IF I COULD.

AND I TOTALLY COULD.

BUT I WON'T.

YOU UNDERSTAND, DON'T YOU?

YEAH, ACTUALLY, I DO.

I MUST MAKE THIS JOURNEY ALONE.

I MUST TRAVEL DOWN, DEEP...

...AS DEEP BELOW AS THE HEAVENS ABOVE ARE HIGH.

I CAN'T WAIT TO SEE ALL MY LOVED ONES AGAIN!

I'LL BRING THEM ALL BACK WITH ME! BACK FROM THEIR UNJUST ENDS!

THROUGH ME, DEATH WILL BE DEAD!

THE RIVER STYX.

SO MANY SOULS...

THIS MIGHT BE TRICKIER TO NAVIGATE THAN I THOUGHT.

INO? ARE YOU HERE?

—A SATYR, WITH FRECKLES. HAS ANYONE SEEN HIM?

MAYBE THEY'RE ON THE OTHER SIDE OF THE STYX. I NEED TO—

THIS IS AS FAR AS YOU CAN GO, DIONYSOS.

HADES! AND PERSEPHONE!

YOU ARE TO BE COMMENDED, NEPHEW. YOU HAVE TRAVELED FAR—AS FAR AS ANY LIVING BEING CAN TRAVEL.

ONLY MY QUEEN, MYSELF, AND HERMES PSYCHOPOMPOS CAN FREELY GO FARTHER.

FOR THE SHADES OF THE RECENTLY DEAD, THE RIVER STYX CAN ONLY BE TRAVERSED BY A RIDE WITH CHARON THE FERRYMAN.

THAT IS A PATH NO LIVING BEING, GOD OR OTHERWISE, CAN TAKE.

ON THE OTHER SIDE OF THE STYX IS THE RIVER LETHE.

TO DRINK OF THE WATERS OF THE LETHE IS TO FORGET WHO YOU ARE, AND THAT IS EXACTLY WHAT THE SHADES THAT CROSS THE STYX DO.

THEY ARE REBORN ANEW, BUT EVERYTHING THEY WERE, EVERYTHING THEY KNEW, ALL THEIR LOVES, HOPES, AND DREAMS—THEY ARE ALL WASHED AWAY.

EVEN IF YOU COULD CROSS THE STYX, TO BRING THEM BACK WOULD BE POINTLESS. THEY ARE NO LONGER THE PEOPLE YOU KNEW.

...SO I'M TOO LATE?

EVERYONE WHO DIED—MY BROTHERS, INO... AMPELOS? THEY'RE REALLY GONE?

ACTUALLY...

THERE IS SOMEONE HERE YOU CAN HELP.

YOU SEE, WHEN SOMEONE DIES, IT IS NOT A FREE TRIP ACROSS THE STYX.

THEY NEED A COIN AS PAYMENT FOR CHARON TO CROSS.

A PERSON'S LOVED ONES TYPICALLY PLACE THE COIN IN THE MOUTH OF THE DECEASED.

BUT WHAT IF THERE'S NO COIN?

NO ONE LEFT A COIN FOR HER. HER FAMILY THOUGHT SHE SIMPLY DISAPPEARED.

IN TRUTH, THERE WAS NOTHING LEFT OF HER TO LEAVE A COIN IN.

DIONYSOS, MEET YOUR MOTHER.

YOU KNOW THIS STORY ALREADY.

GAEA BEGAT OURANOS, THE SKY.

GAEA MADE OURANOS HER HUSBAND, AND HE FATHERED HER CHILDREN, THE TITANS, THE GODS OF TIME.

AND THE TITANS OVERTHREW OURANOS.

AND THE TITANS BEGAT THE OLYMPIANS, AND THE OLYMPIANS OVERTHREW THE TITANS.

WE SET OURSELVES ABOVE THE HUMANS, ON THRONES IN PALACES IN THE SKY.

WE OLYMPIANS ARE ETERNAL. PERFECT. UNDYING.

SO MUCH OF WHAT IT MEANS TO BE HUMAN WILL FOREVER BE DENIED US.

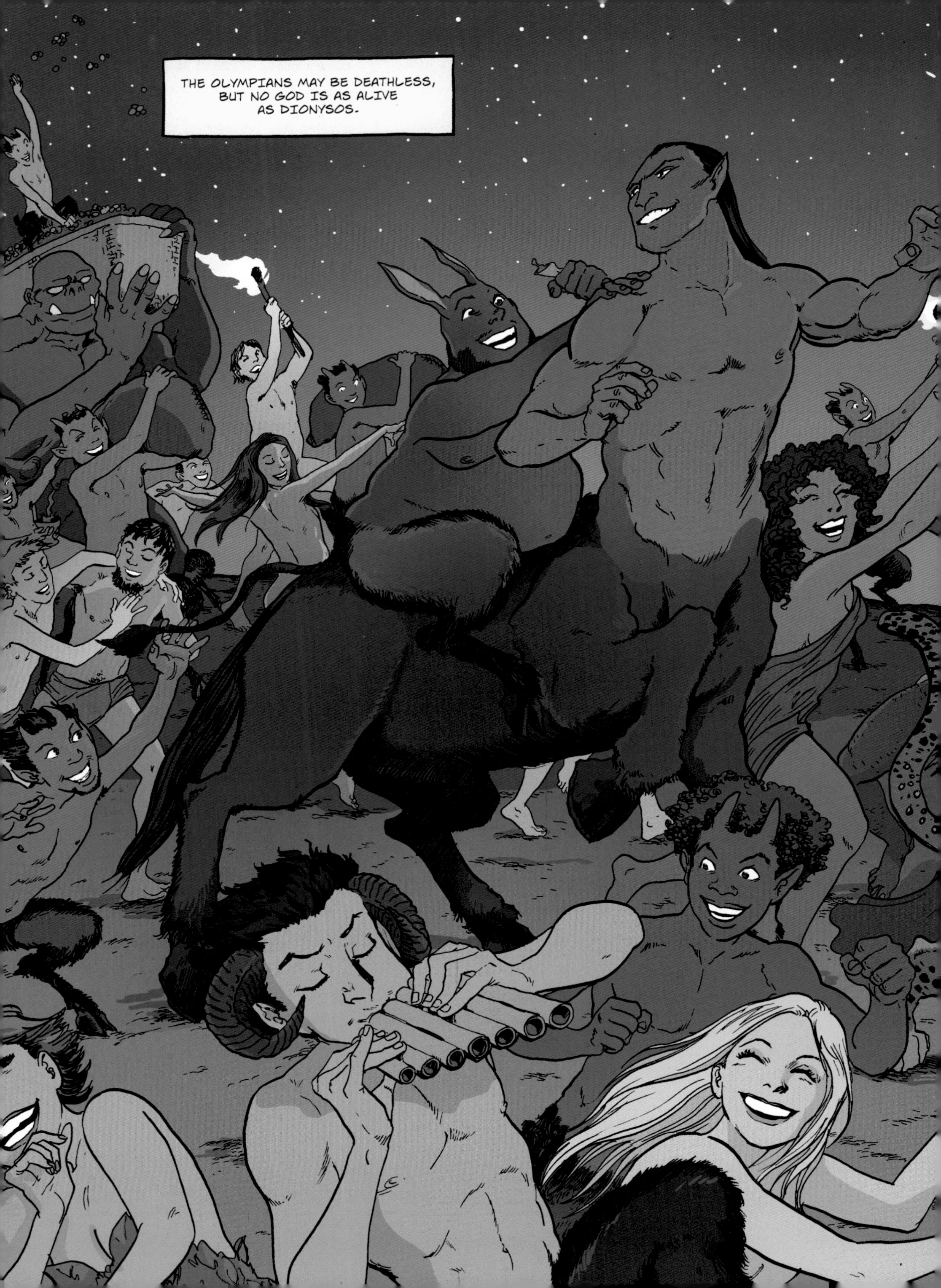
THE OLYMPIANS MAY BE DEATHLESS, BUT NO GOD IS AS ALIVE AS DIONYSOS.

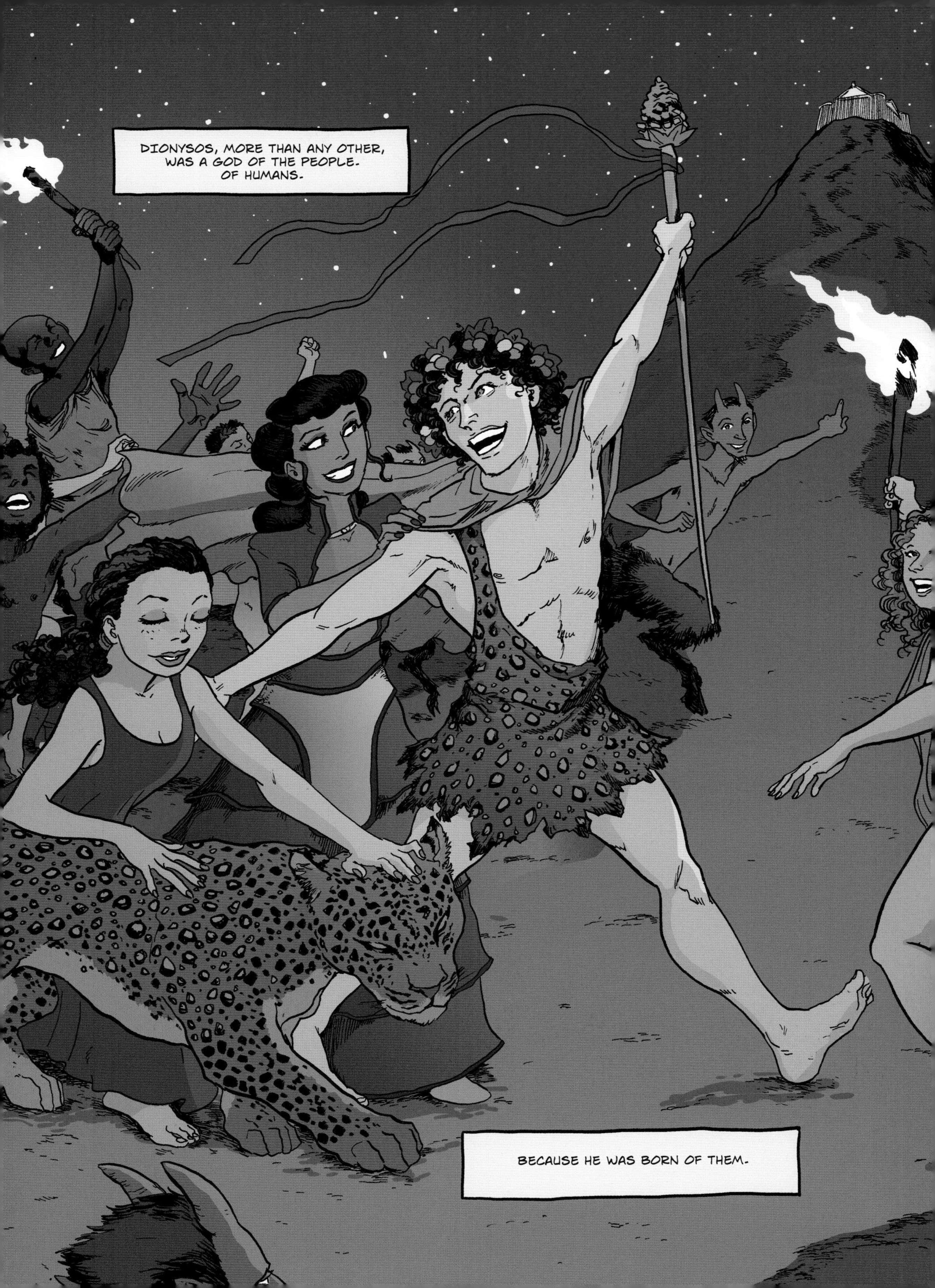
DIONYSOS, MORE THAN ANY OTHER, WAS A GOD OF THE PEOPLE. OF HUMANS.
BECAUSE HE WAS BORN OF THEM.

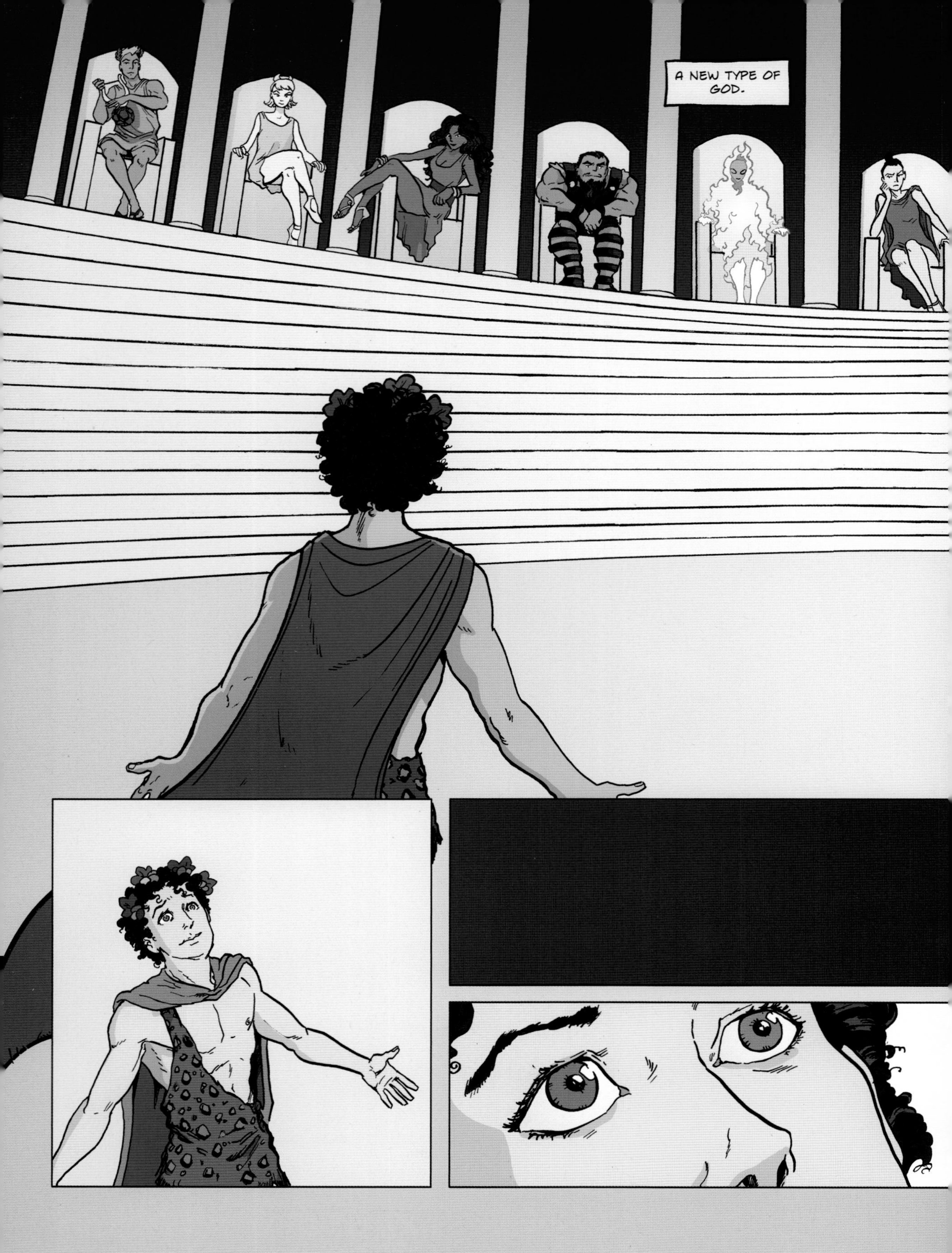
A NEW TYPE OF GOD.

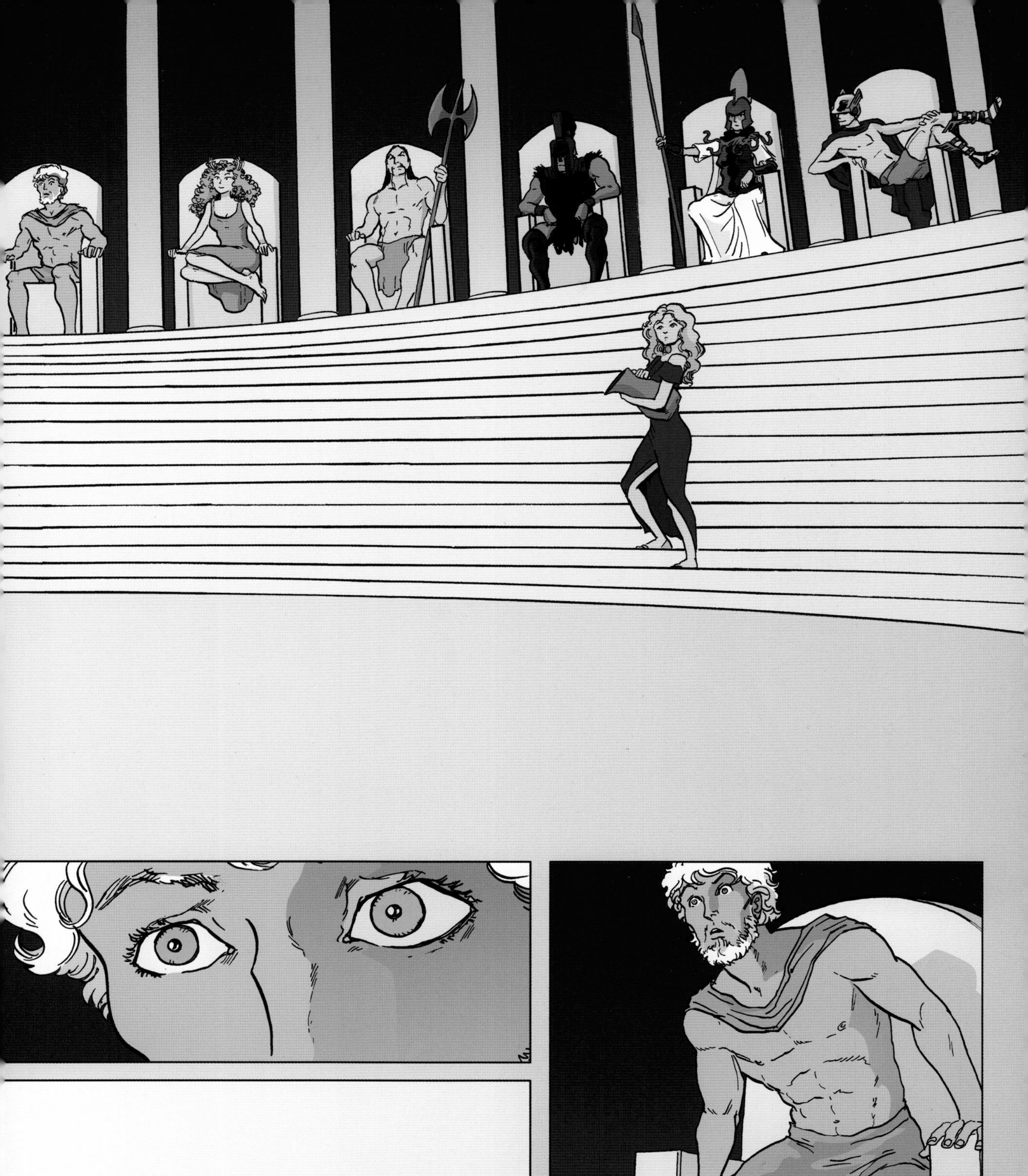

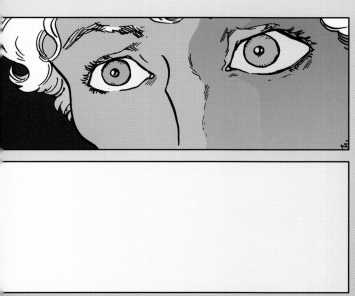

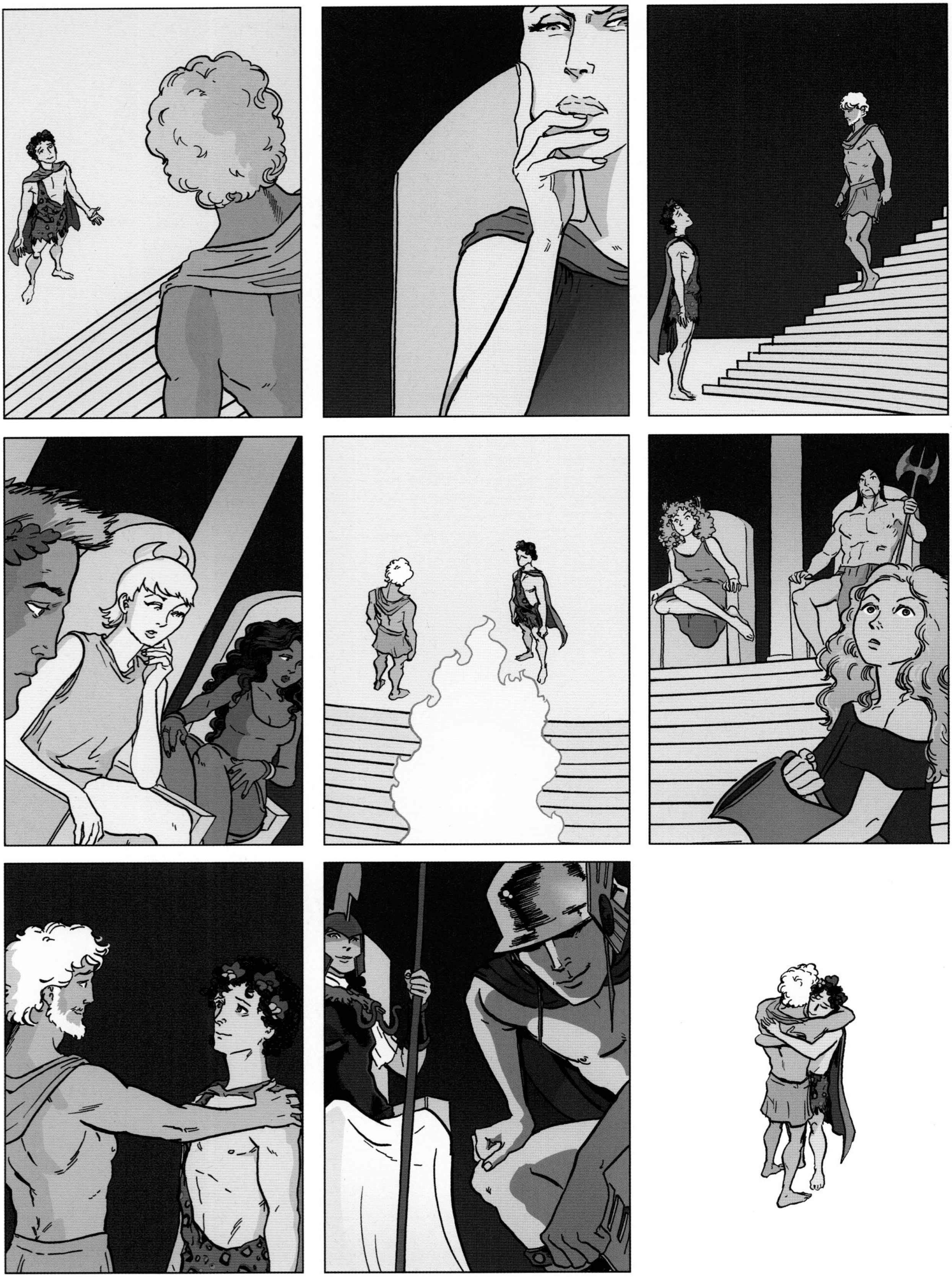

GREETINGS, O SON OF ZEUS.

WE'VE ALL BEEN HEARING QUITE A LOT ABOUT YOU.

ALL YOUR DEEDS AND ADVENTURES. OF THIS FOLLOWING YOU'VE CREATED FOR YOURSELF.

EVEN HOW YOU'VE CONQUERED DEATH!

TERRIBLY IMPRESSIVE, ALL OF IT. REALLY.

AND WE HEAR YOU WISH TO JOIN US HERE, TO TAKE A THRONE ON OLYMPUS!

SUCH AMBITION IS SURELY TO BE ADMIRED!

THERE'S JUST ONE TINY PROBLEM.

THERE ARE ONLY TWELVE THRONES.

WE *COULD* ADD ANOTHER, BUT IT WOULD UPSET THE SYMMETRY. YOU UNDERSTAND.

TO OFFER YOU A THRONE, SOMEONE ELSE WOULD HAVE TO GIVE UP THEIRS.

ANY OFFERS?

ANYONE AT ALL?

I DIDN'T THINK SO. I'M SO VERY SORRY, DIONYSUS, BUT YOU'LL JUST HA—

WELCOME, DIONYSOS. I KEPT YOUR SEAT WARM FOR YOU.

HESTIA, YOU SURRENDER YOUR THRONE? TO HIM?

A—ARE YOU LEAVING?

NO!

NO, OF COURSE NOT. YOU ARE MY FAMILY.

I'VE JUST NEVER FELT AT HOME ON A THRONE.

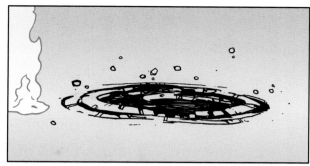

THIS WILL BE MY SEAT NOW.

AND I GUESS THIS WILL BE MINE! A BIT AUSTERE, BUT COMFY.

SYMMETRY PRESERVED AND EVERYTHING! MANY THANKS, AUNT HESTIA!

SO, I SUPPOSE THAT'S SETTLED, THEN.

I SUPPOSE...?

SIIIGH.

I SUPPOSE.

I NEED SOME WATER. HEBE?

UM, ACTUALLY, CAN I MAKE A SUGGESTION?

AH, I WONDER IF WE MIGHT TRY A LITTLE SOMETHING NEW? SOMETHING OF MY OWN CREATION?

THANK YOU, HEBE.

AND A TOAST, IF I MAY.

TO THE OLYMPIANS: LONG MAY THEY REIGN!

HMM.

HMM...

SO...

SO...

SO... HAVE YOU ALL HEARD ABOUT THIS GUY SISYPHUS? OH, MAN, THIS STORY IS NUTS!

GO ON...

THERE HAD BEEN TWELVE OLYMPIANS— TWELVE PERFECT, IMPERFECT GODS, LIVING IN ASSUMED HUMAN FORMS.

MY FAMILY.

CHANGING AND GROWING, LAUGHING AND LOVING, FIGHTING AND FLIRTING.

ALL AROUND ME THEY GATHER, AND OLD TALES ARE TOLD. NEW STORIES UNFOLD.

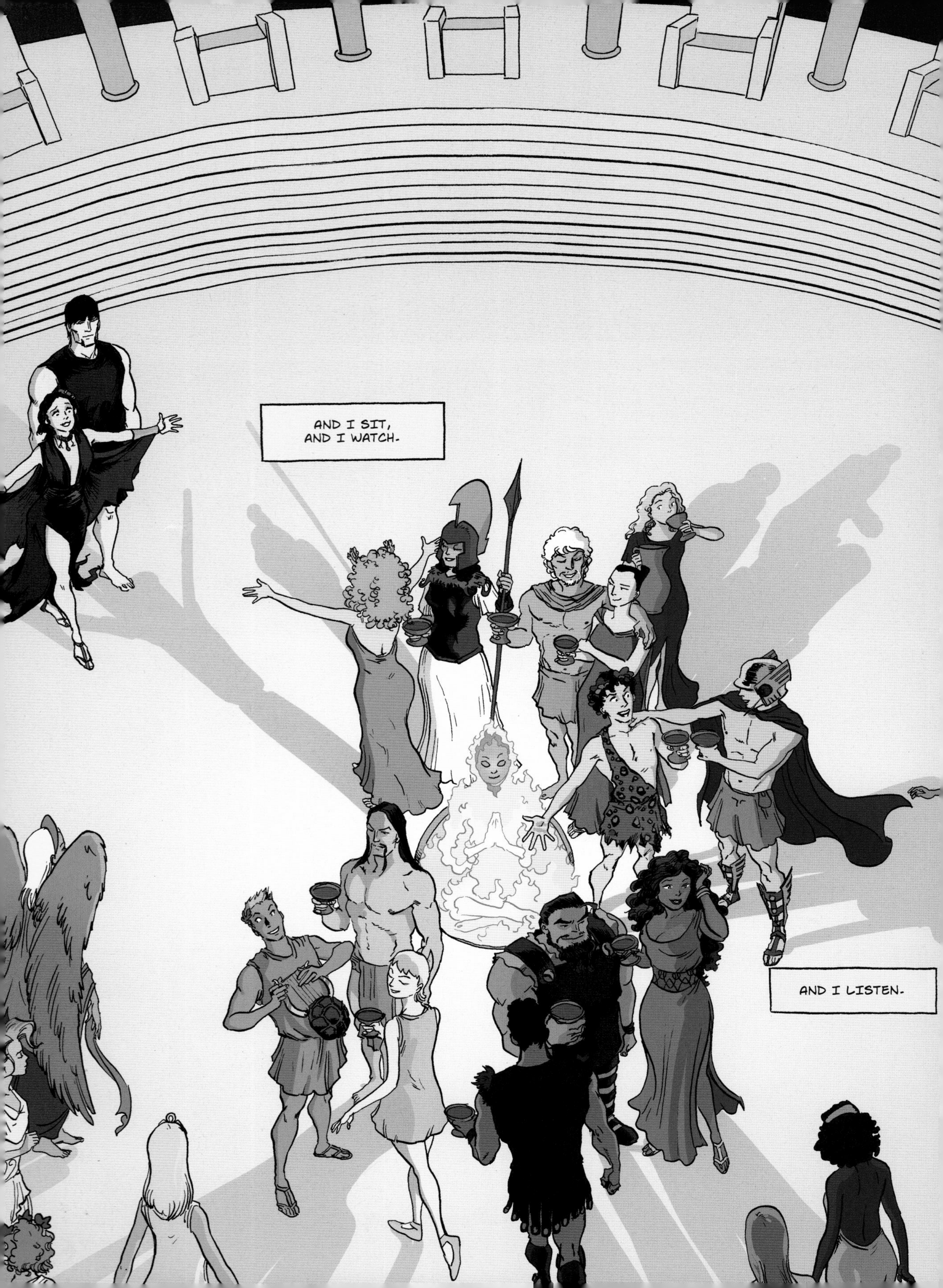
AND I SIT,
AND I WATCH.
AND I LISTEN.

### Where to end?

More than ten years ago, in the first volume of OLYMPIANS, I began my author's note with a question: Where to start? It only makes sense that now, as the series draws to a conclusion, I ask the bookend question.

Dionysos was the last Olympian, the youngest of the Gods, and moreover, a new type of God—born of a mortal woman. The ascension of Dionysos heralded a new age, a new way for humankind to think about our deities. For all those reasons, since I first began working on this series, I always knew it would end with Dionysos—well, in an ideal world at least.

OLYMPIANS could have bombed and ended unceremoniously somewhere, anywhere, along the way, like with *Hades* or *Artemis* or whomever. But it didn't. You, the readers, embraced my take on the Greek Gods in a way I could only have dreamt of and allowed me to craft a twelve-volume series about them. OLYMPIANS is the series I always wished I could read when I was introduced to Greek mythology, and I got to create it. That's pretty huge, literally a life's work, and I have all of you to thank for it. I raise a glass to you all—metaphorically, that is. I don't even like wine (sacrilege to say, in a book about Dionysos, I know).

And not just the readers, but to all the people who have helped bring this series to life—too many people to list by name here (not to mention I'll undoubtedly overlook someone vitally important). So, to everyone at First Second and Macmillan, I raise a glass. To all my friends, family, and loved ones, a glass. To my proofreaders, my flatters, everyone who ever took the time to drop me a line, a glass. To everyone I overlooked, a glass.

And finally, let me raise a glass to the Gods themselves, and the world that created them, this wonderful, wild, insane family that's captured the fascination of me and countless others like me. I couldn't ask for a better set of Muses.

To quote Dionysos, in a toast he makes in this very volume, "To the Olympians: Long may they reign!" I raise a glass.

And I don't even like wine.

George O'Connor
Brooklyn, NY
2021

# DIONYSOS
## MAKER OF MERRY AND MADNESS

**GOD OF** Wine, Drunkenness, Frenzy, Disorder, Theater, Madness; he was also a principal God of the Mysteries, an offshoot of Ancient Greek religion with a focus on a blessed afterlife.

**OTHER NAME** Bacchus, (in the Mysteries) Zagreus

**ROMAN NAME** Liber, Liber Pater

**SYMBOLS** Grapes, Vines, Thrysos (a type of wand topped by a pine cone), Masks, Chalice

**SACRED ANIMALS** Leopard, Dolphin, Serpent, Ram

**SACRED PLANTS** Grapevine (duh), Ivy, Pine Tree

**SACRED PLACES** Mount Nysa (site of his childhood with the Satyrs), Naxos (where he met his wife, Ariadne), Eleusis (principal site of the Mysteries), Theater of Dionysos (Athens)

**HEAVENLY BODIES** 3671 Dionysus and 2063 Bacchus, both asteroids

**MODERN LEGACY** A particularly wild party will still be referred to as a bacchanal.

Some elements of the worship of Dionysos can still be found in the major religions of today.

# G<sup>R</sup>EEK NOTES

PAGE 1: "You know this story already"—if you're a longtime reader of OLYMPIANS this is definitely true. I've retold this story of creation before, most notably in Book 1 of OLYMPIANS, *Zeus: King of the Gods*, and then again in Book 6, *Aphrodite: Goddess of Love*. (In fact, both of those volumes open with the same first line as the book you're holding now.) The story of the Greek Gods is often a cyclical one, and I felt I should bring it back to where it started for the final volume.

PAGE 6, PANEL 1: This "stillborn" child is actually the stone effigy substituted for baby Zeus by Rhea and Gaea in OLYMPIANS Book 1, *Zeus: King of the Gods*.

PAGE 6, PANELS 3–5: For a look at what Poseidon dreamt about in the void, please see OLYMPIANS Book 5, *Poseidon: Earth Shaker*.

PAGES 7–9: For a view of these events from another angle, check out OLYMPIANS Book 1, *Zeus: King of the Gods*.

PAGE 10, PANEL 3: Speaking of different angles, this is the group shot of the OG Olympians from the back cover of every volume of this series, redrawn from Hestia's perspective.

PAGE 11, PANEL 2: "The tallest mountain left standing"—a variation on that line appears in every volume of OLYMPIANS, with the exception of *Hera: The Goddess and Her Glory*, a book that also just happens to be perhaps my personal favorite. COINCIDENCE?! You be the judge.

PAGE 12, PANEL 3: Boy, families can be rough, huh?

PAGE 13, PANEL 2: Seriously, no one should talk about Priapos.

PAGE 13, PANEL 4: This is my imagining of the colossal statue of Zeus at Olympia, sculpted by Phidias, one of the seven Ancient Wonders of the World. This seated statue was more than forty feet tall and made of gold and ivory. The statue is completely lost to us now—all that survives is a fairly extensive description by history's first travel guide writer, Pausanias, and some rather crude reproductions of the statue's general pose on some old coins.

PAGE 15, PANEL 7: Semele here is referencing some of Zeus's other famous conquests—he took the form of a shower of gold to seduce Danae, mother of Perseus (see OLYMPIANS Book 2, *Athena: Grey-eyed Goddess*), and a swan for Leda, mother of Helen and the twins Castor and Polydeuces, the Dioscuri.

PAGE 16, PANELS 3–4: Hera (you did realize that the old lady is Hera in disguise, didn't you?) makes reference to her own seduction by Zeus (as seen in OLYMPIANS Book 3, *Hera: The Goddess and Her Glory*). The ant is my nod to perhaps the strangest of Zeus's conquests—he fathered the ancestor of the Myrmidons (the nation Achilles hails from) in the form of an ant. An ant! It's best not to think about it.

PAGE 19: Among the many duties of Hermes is the responsibility to escort the recently deceased to the Underworld (see *Hades: Lord of the Dead* and *Hermes: Tales of the Trickster*, among others). Also, I gotta say, as a superhero nerd, it makes all kinds of sense to me in a comic book sort of way that the true form of an Olympian is essentially a miniature sun. Jack Kirby would approve.

PAGE 21, PANEL 5: Very occasionally, in creating OLYMPIANS, there is a concept so strange that I am unable to think of a way to satisfyingly depict it without looking ridiculous. Dionysos being born from the thigh of Zeus is one of those, so I hearkened back to an original depiction. This panel is liberally adapted from a fourth century BCE krater (a sort of vessel that wine was mixed in).

PAGE 22, PANEL 1: Hermes's pose here is an homage to a famous statue of Hermes by Praxiteles. Praxiteles was the most famous sculptor of his day, and the Hermes is (perhaps) the only statue of his that survives to the present.

PAGE 22, PANEL 5: Little girl Dionysos is the most adorable Dionysos.

PAGE 23, PANEL 5: Hermes's pose here, carrying Dionysos as a lamb, is in reference to a style of ancient statue called a kriophoros, or "ram bearer."

PAGE 24, PANEL 3: Little Dionysos (now a boy) retains wee tiny stubbins of horns from his time disguised as a lamb. This is a reference to a tradition among some ancient sources that depict Dionysos with ram horns. References! References everywhere! HAHAHAHA!

PAGE 24, PANEL 5: Easiest game of Where's Waldo ever.

PAGE 25: I have had the same reaction as the snake to the taste of wine.

PAGE 26: Interestingly, I've also had the same reaction as Silenos to wine.

PAGE 27, PANEL 4: You can witness the strange head-birth of Athena yourself in OLYMPIANS Book 2, *Athena: Grey-Eyed Goddess*.

PAGE 28, PANEL 3: Like father, like son. To see what I mean, check out OLYMPIANS Book 1, *Zeus: King of the Gods*. Cyclical!

PAGE 30: Ampelos's name means "grapevine," ironic given his demise but appropriate for the first love of the God of wine.

PAGE 32, PANEL 1: Stan Lee famously said to write every comic with the idea it was going to be the first comic someone ever read. I normally try to write every volume of OLYMPIANS with that supposition in mind—ideally, you can read the series in any order and it should all make sense. However, if this book is the first volume of OLYMPIANS you've ever read you're probably all like "Who is this lady talking to Zeus from the darkness? Did I miss something? WHAT IS GOING ON?!" Let me alleviate your confusion by saying this is Metis, first wife of Zeus and mother of Athena. She helped Zeus overthrow the Titans and he swallowed her for her trouble. She now lives in Zeus's head. The boy she's talking about, who hears advice when he puts his head to Grandmother Earth? IT'S ZEUS HIMSELF! Everything is cyclical!

PAGE 32, PANEL 5: What's this, you ask? Bearded Dionysos is yet another reference to a tradition in ancient art to depict him that way? YOU DON'T SAY.

PAGE 33, PANEL 4: If you can't read Cyrillic, that tombstone says "Ikarios." Yikes.

PAGE 33, PANEL 5: In some versions of the story of Lycurgus, his big beef with the God of Wine is that Lycurgus was a beer drinker. I didn't go that route, but as a nod to it I drew hops, the plant from which beer is brewed, on the shields of Lycurgus's army.

PAGE 36, PANEL 9: *Arrested Development* reference! To read further adventures of King Midas, please go to my website (www.georgeoconnorbooks.com) and sign up for my mailing list. You will be automatically sent the free digital-only OLYMPIANS story, "The Ears of King Midas."

PAGE 37, PANEL 6: Thetis was fated to give birth to a child who would be greater than his father. Zeus and Poseidon both almost became that dad in OLYMPIANS Book 6, *Aphrodite: Goddess of Love*.

PAGE 42, PANEL 4: Now you know why dolphins are so smart! They used to be people!

PAGE 43, PANEL 8: If you're paying attention you might be thinking "Now wait a second . . . Dionysos's mom, Semele, was a princess of Thebes. Dionysos just used his powers of madness to make the women of Thebes tear apart Pentheus, the king of Thebes. Did Dionysos just kill his own grandpa?" Worry not! With the deaths of Semele and her sister Ino that specific branch of the family tree ended and kingship of Thebes passed on to their nephew, Pentheus. So Dionsyos didn't kill his grandpa, he just murdered his cousin. That's way better, right? Right?

PAGE 44, PANEL 5: The daughter of Demeter and Zeus, Persephone, is supposed to spend the fall and winter in the Underworld with her husband, Hades, and spring and summer on Olympus with her ma. Read all about this deal in OLYMPIANS Book 4, *Hades: Lord of the Dead*.

PAGE 45, PANEL 3: More art references? DON'T MIND IF I DO! The images of frolicking porpoises and youths somersaulting over the horns of bulls come from the famous frescoes discovered at the Minoan palace of Knossos. We last saw Princess Ariadne herself in OLYMPIANS Book 5, *Poseidon: Earth Shaker*. She's talking here about Theseus, grade A creep and son of Poseidon.

PAGE 46, PANELS 1–3: For the music, my original script says "Some sort of indication of music, and distant sound." Now clearly I can't write that in the final book, but a little research revealed the series of symbols Ancient Greeks used to represent music. This is the culmination of my clumsy attempt to write ancient Grecian musical notation, drawn in a fashion meant to be indicative of the feeling of music ebbing and flowing. The composition depicted, by the way, is the "Seiklos Epitaph," the oldest surviving complete musical composition in the world. The lyrics to this song previously appeared in OLYMPIANS Book 10, *Hermes: Tales of the Trickster*.

PAGE 49: No need for sunblock, Zeus, Aphrodite is throwing all the shade you need.

PAGE 52: Poor Ares. All he wanted was a big fight, and then the whole thing happened in Lysurgus's head. Also, given that Lysurgus means "oak" and considering what he did to his own legs, does that make Lysurgus a lumber-jack? Also also, if you tell a joke in *Geek Notes* and no one laughs, did it actually happen?

PAGE 53: More echoes of his father from Dionysos here. The Goddess handing Dio a torch is Hekate, last seen serving as a guide to Demeter in *Hades: Lord of the Dead*. In case you're wondering why an amphibian is cluttering up the foreground of panel 8, that's a reference to the comedy *The Frogs* by Aristophanes, about Dionysos's journeying to the Underworld.

PAGE 56, PANELS 3–5: As the trickster God of magic, lies, and money, of course Hermes is going to be good at coin tricks.

PAGE 57: Cyclical, I tell you, cyclical!

PAGE 62: Comics are awesome, words and pictures coming together in a glorious alchemy to tell a story. Sometimes, though, you just gotta shut up and let the pictures do all the work.

PAGE 67, PANEL 1: I chose the tale of Sisyphus to be the story Hermes tells because (A) it legit can be hilarious (just check out Hephaistos doing a spit take at some unheard punch line), and (B) it's a story I never got to tell in OLYMPIANS (though we briefly met Sisyphus in *Hades: Lord of the Dead*). That said, it is a story I retold, in a non-OLYMPIANS way, in the terrific anthology graphic novel *Comics Squad: Recess*. Check it out, George O'Connor completists!

PAGE 67, PANEL 3: Last art reference, I promise! The layout of this panel pays homage to a not-particularly-well-known painting by a not-enormously-well-known painter named Giovanni Antonio "Lo Spadarino" Galli entitled *Convito degli Dei (Feast of the Gods)*. I came upon it wandering through the Uffizi in Florence years ago and have always loved it and the moment of Olympians family revelry it captured. Look it up, if you can!

PAGE 68: Boy, families can be awesome, huh?

And that's a wrap! Thanks for joining me on a journey through the Greekier aspects of Mythic Greece!

# HESTIA
## FIRST OF THE OLYMPIANS

**GODDESS OF** Fire, the Hearth, the Home

**ROMAN NAME** Vesta

**SACRED PLANT** Oak, Chaste Tree

**SACRED PLACES** Hestia had very few temples in Ancient Greece; instead, every fireplace in every home was regarded as her shrine. That said, there were sanctuaries dedicated to her in Olympia and Sparta, among other places.

**MONTH** December

**HEAVENLY BODIES** Vesta, a minor planet; and 46 Hestia, an asteroid

**MODERN LEGACY** As a deity with almost no attendant mythology, who was rarely personified in art and lacking any easy-to-identify physical characteristics, Hestia is a comparatively little-known figure today, despite being the firstborn Olympian and an enormously important figure in Olympian religions. Let's fix this, huh? Spread the word of Hestia!

# ABOUT THIS BOOK

**DIONYSIS: THE NEW GOD** is the twelfth book in OLYMPIANS, a graphic novel series from First Second that retells the Greek myths.

# FOR DISCUSSION

**1** This is the twelfth book of OLYMPIANS. Much is made in the story of the importance of there being twelve thrones on Olympus. But there are more than twelve Olympians. Why do you think the number twelve is so important?

**2** Why do you think Hestia took a human form upon her birth?

**3** If you had one wish from Zeus, sworn on the River Styx, like Semele did, what would you ask for?

**4** There is a lot in this book about the true forms of characters: Zeus was made to reveal his, with disastrous consequences; Hestia takes a human-like form but hides it beneath a sheath of flames; Dionysos was born a girl, became a boy, and spent some time as a ram (!) in between. Which of these is the true form of Dionysos? If you could take any shape, what would be your true form?

**5** If Dionysos gave you the power to transform everything you touched, what would you want to be able to turn things into?

**6** The Olympians are a big crazy family. How does your family match up to the Olympians?

**7** Dionysos travels to the Underworld to meet his mother. What famous deceased person would you most want to meet?

**8** Dionysos decides to become the God of Wine. What would you be the Goddess or God of?

**9** Very few people believe in the Greek Gods today. Why do you think it's important we still learn about them?

# BIBLIOGRAPHY

**HESIOD: VOLUME 1, THEOGENY. WORKS AND DAYS: TESTIMONIA.**
**NEW YORK: LOEB CLASSICAL LIBRARY, 2007.**
Hesiod is the foundation upon which OLYMPIANS has been constructed and this volume is no exception. All the Hestia stuff comes from here.

**APOLLODORUS, THE LIBRARY, TRANSLATED BY J. G. FRAZER, VOLUME 1.**
**NEW YORK: LOEB CLASSICAL LIBRARY, 1921.**
This was my main source for the stories of Semele and Lycurgus. And the trip to the Underworld. And the bit about a crazy Dionysos wandering around the desert. Basically everything. Also it's written by pseudo-Apollodorus, which makes me laugh.

**OVID, FASTI.**
**NEW YORK: PENGUIN CLASSICS, 2000.**
This was a pretty good source, albeit somewhat short, for Dionysos's lost first love, Ampelos.

**OVID, METAMORPHOSES.**
**NEW YORK: PENGUIN CLASSICS, 2004.**
I used this as the primary account for my retelling of the pirates and the fate of King Pentheus of Thebes. Ovid was Roman, so he uses the Roman names for the Greek Gods, but he mostly calls Dionysos Bacchus, which works for both Greek and Roman, so it's pretty much a win-win for me here.

**THEOI GREEK MYTHOLOGY WEBSITE WWW.THEOI.COM**
Without a doubt, the single most valuable resource I came across in this entire venture. At theoi.com, you can find an encyclopedia of various Gods and Goddesses from Greek mythology, cross-referenced with every mention of them in hundreds of ancient Greek and Roman texts. Unfortunately, it's not quite complete, and it doesn't seem to be updated anymore.

**WWW.THEOI.COM/LIBRARY.HTML**
A subsection of the above site, it's an online archive of hundreds of ancient Greek and Roman texts. Many of these have never been published in the traditional sense, and many are just fragments recovered from ancient papyrus or recovered text from other authors' quotations of lost epics. Invaluable.

# ALSO RECOMMENDED
## FOR YOUNGER READERS

*D'Aulaires' Book of Greek Myths.* Ingri and Edgar Parin D'Aulaire. New York: Doubleday, 1962.

## FOR OLDER READERS

*The Marriage of Cadmus and Harmony.* Robert Calasso. New York: Knopf, 1993.

*Mythology.* Edith Hamilton. New York: Grand Central Publishing, 1999.

*Dionysos: Archetypal Image of the Indestructible Life.* Carl Kerenyi. Prin

*A toast. To everyone who helped see these books to completion, to all my loved ones, to everyone who supported this series, more people than I could ever list here—this book is for you. And of course, I raise a glass to the Olympians themselves—that family of perfect, imperfect Gods, living in assumed human forms—long may you reign.*

—G. O.

Firs† Second

Published by First Second
First Second is an imprint of Roaring Brook Press,
a division of Holtzbrinck Publishing Holdings Limited Partnership
120 Broadway, New York, NY 10271
firstsecondbooks.com
mackids.com

Library of Congress Cataloging-in-Publication Data is available.

Our books may be purchased in bulk for promotional, educational, or business use.
Please contact your local bookseller or the Macmillan Corporate and Premium Sales Department
at (800) 221-7945 ext. 5442 or by email at MacmillanSpecialMarkets@macmillan.com.

First edition, 2022
Edited by Mark Siegel and Kiara Valdez
Cover design by Danica Novgorodoff
Interior book design by Molly Johanson and Madeline Morales

Printed in China by Toppan Leefung Printing Ltd., Dongguan City, Guangdong Province

ISBN 978-1-62672-531-7 (paperback)
10 9 8 7 6 5 4 3 2 1

ISBN 978-1-62672-530-0 (hardcover)
10 9 8 7 6 5 4 3 2 1

Don't miss your next favorite book from First Second!
For the latest updates go to firstsecondnewsletter.com and sign up for our enewsletter.